EXCERPT Magazine No. 3
Copyright ©2025
ISBN: 978-0-9855180-5-9
www.excerptmag.com

Excerpts from *Twilight of the Gods* (Stalking Horse Press, 2025)
and *The Slapjack* (Black Rose Writing, 2025)
printed with permission from the presses

EDITOR'S NOTE

Dear Reader,

We invite you into these pages, these excerpts, these six fictive dreams from novels published and unpublished, as an escape, yes, but also proof that this luminant prismatic looking glass we call "art" matters. You will be transported on a journey from a small town in the Great Depression to Golden Age Hollywood to a 1980s newsroom at the Arizona Tribune and the football fields of Cactus Basin, Texas, entering the hearts and minds of human characters, wholly imagined into existence like a magic trick.

How marvelous is that? Teleportation, reflection, investigation, dramatization of this very messy life, dredging the subconscious for some fleeting comprehension, perhaps some ineffable epiphany, of what it means to be human, grasping at the furtive truth like fish in a stream through the stories we tell ourselves. Moreover, an analogy experience, a book!, a refuge from the digital idiocy of our current age, living like functioning lunatics between two worlds, one of which is now controlled almost entirely by a fascist broligarchy that seems intent on turning us into frightened, obedient little robots with our values, opinions, choices (moral, spiritual, economic) reduced to 1s and 0s. You are more than any binary, data set, or voting block. You are human. You are here on a marvelous blue dot in the infinite cosmos, reading words on a page written by another human to let you inhabit the worlds, hearts, and inner life of others.

As we find ourselves unable to imagine a way out of the trainwreck nightmare that began with Reagan's moronic free-market wet dream and somehow ends with the rise of techno-feudalism, billionaire man-childs, and the threat of fascism in America, remember that democracy in this country began with the sweep of a fountain pen on a piece of parchment. And a thousand pens are mightier than any wannabe king.

Write. Read. Resist. Divest. Protest. Protect. Strike. This nihilistic late-stage capitalist hamster wheel of ruthless exploitation and oppression may seem unstoppable. But as Ursula Le Guin once said, so did the divine right of kings once upon a time. Keep reading, keep writing, keep imagining. *Nolite te bastardes carborundorum.*

DW Ardern
Editor-in-Chief

EXCERPT MAGAZINE

No. 3   Spring 2025

--- *In This Issue* ---

--- *Masthead* ---

DW Ardern   Editor-in-Chief
Jenny Maattala   Fiction Editor
Cam Terwilliger   Fiction Editor
Isaac High   Assistant Editor
Justin Richel   Cover Artist

THE SLAPJACK

by

ALAN SINCIC

The Claim

Rumor had it Maggie had taken ill, taken to bed on account of GB who'd abandoned her. All of which stirred in Joe a (near to fatherly) concern. Such a burden to carry alone.

A single lantern swung from a nail above the transom, lit the empty shell of the Slapjack, confettied the porch with the shadow of a moth. Maggie'd propped the windows, the three on a side, open, so as to ferry the cool night air over the sill and into the heat of the kitchen. Over a sill (the big one, up front) she'd slung a tablecloth to dry. In the dark of the yard, the brick at the base of the hand-pump shimmered white. Joe could smell the fresh of the paint. From one end of the porch to the other, a coalition of rockers and cane-backs and flimsy wobblers rode up top of one another, locked elbows, tottered over the boy who rode the mop. Magical the hour.

Joe paused at the gate. If he'd had a brake lever to shudder the world to a stop, here would be the place. He straightened his collar and ran his hand atop (without touching) the tin sign that bore the ghost of the old *Royster Feed and Seed*. The word *DINER*, in fat red letters, obliterated the rooster logo and the cursive—like piping on a cake—*Royster*. He could just make out in the glow of the lantern—there beneath a coat of whitewash—a silhouette: *Corn, Chemicals, Twine.*

Coleman Quick Lite, said the lantern, *Sunshine of the Night.* From the air it pulled, ample as the air itself, a steady breath. Infinite the breath. It whispered out in equal measure light, and heat, and the earthy scent of kerosene. Coal. Peat. Iron. Such a wonder. How it could be? A wicker filament size of a thimble lights a tree or a dock or an acre of grain, lights, right up to the rafters, the whole of a barn?

So it goes. From out the acorn, the oak. From out a grifter like Maggie, a palace of griddle cakes and hash-browns and omelets and bacon. It was Maggie broke into the abandoned building, hauled out the rubble, scrounged up a stove and a sink and a counter and a till. She put a cot in the corner and a sign above the door: *Pie.* Maggie the Maker.

He rubbed at the skin on the inside of his wrist, the one and then the other, there, to warm it, where the pulse runs, the invisible charisma of blood, the trace of Russian Leather by L' Aiglon he bought from behind the counter at the Five-and-Dime, top-of-the-line elixir framed by a cardboard print of a Cossack Horseman and the slogan *Scents and Such for the Hairy-Chested.*

And the hat. Hat in hand. Joe had him a weather hat for when the heaven beat the earth and a fair-weather hat for when the heaven behaved. The hats were identical in every way. Size six and a quarter derby in midnight blue, and up in the hollow where the head goes, on a ceiling of silk at the height of the dome, an embossment in gold foil, a pair of old-timey lions, like outta Robin Hood, like outta Sherwood

Forest. The hatter he pictured. Tiny man with calipers and scissors and a ball-peen hammer—he dampers with the skin of a baby deer. To the gunwale the hatter hammers a little fly of fabric so's you don't wear it backwards, and at a cocky angle he snaps the brim, and into the brown leather sweat-band he punches the seal of the patent, *Improved Cavanagh Edge 1805977.*

Identical, these two hats belonging to Joe, the difference being (as in all things human) the wear. No way around it. You wear a cap to impress, but the minute you wear it, it's a wear on the cap. When the wind bullies and the rain volleys and the sun like a sledgehammer lands, you wear the weather cap, sure—*shabby-genteel* the word, like the Parthenon, elegant even on the road to ruin—but when the sky clears? Ah. That's the moment.

Which is why he never wore the fair-weather hat. He would carry it (careful not to warp the brim) in his left hand, as a token of command, and he would always, at the end of the day, or at a change in the weather, return it to the box—the wooden hatbox, the Ark of the Covenant, black and octagonal, and carved as if out of a honeycomb, and with a garnish of gold, and stamped with the logo of the Dobbs and Company, Fifth Avenue. The stamp on the box the capper: a carriage with a coachman up top, a whip and a horse and a top hat, the whole deal.

He crossed the dark yard and up the steps to the lip of the porch. On the way there he'd managed to assemble him-self, a limp and a story to go with it. Portable story. When she would ask, he would shrug, and say it was nothing. *No price too high to pay* he'd say.

What? she'd say. *What do you mean?*

It's nothing he'd say. *Don't mention it.*

No – what? she'd say. *What do you mean?*

So then he'd have to tell her. He was a veteran, see, combat veteran, survivor of the battle of the Marne. He would look out the window. Into the distance. A harbor. Silver in the gloaming as the seed of a pumpkin, there, on the horizon, a ship. *Ta-ra-ra Boom-de-ay* they sing—the sailors, arm-in-arm with the soldiers, arm-in-arm with the cabin boys and the mess cooks and the nurses and the captain (brisk as a bon-bonniere in his almondy whites and sealed with rivets of royal icing yellow as the yolk of an egg) sing, they sing as they slide off over the edge of the earth and away.

What was it like? she'd say.

The trenches, he'd say, and pause. *The Hun.*

She'd lay her hand on his. He'd make as if to clench the fist and then, of a sudden, pause. Through the palm of her hand, the beat of his heart would travel. Breathless. She would be breathless.

The gas, he would say. *The chlorine. The phosgene. The mustard.*

Think of it. Picture it. And she would. She would picture it. They would picture it together. Joe, sensitive Joe, day in and day out all sooty as a ham in the midst of that deadly contagion and even—he would tell her in a husky voice—he was even, to this day, allergic to even so much as a whiff of mustard. He'd hint how GB'd deliberately, and with malice aforethought, seeded the ground with a tincture of Gulden's so as to render Joe, and at the height of the duel, and for all intents and purposes, blind as a peeled potato.

Joe stepped out of the shadows and made for the door. The boy dropped the bucket and scurried away. Stick of a kid she paid a quarter a day to fetch and to carry, shadow up beside her as she tooled around town with a basket of pies or dickered with the miller or scavenged away at the landfill for the saleable loot and the fixable treasure. Sparrow, she called him. Typical woman. So scared of a man, she makes a pet of—not that Joe'd be jealous of a boy. Barefoot boy with a pocky face and shred of a shirt and—look at him run. Run from Joe. Force of personality they call it, the way Joe carried himself. How much bigger he felt in the company of smaller beings. And there was more. A feeling he would never name, even to himself, on account of, well, on account of pride. To be with a broken woman, to feel bigger on account of that. He would always be the stronger, the straighter. And the broken building —the Slap-Dash he called it—made him feel even that much bigger. Leave it to Maggie make a bronze medallion from out the petrified patty of a cow. Women. Torture a T-square to find a angle true. Women!

Wrapped in a sheet is where he found Maggie, propped on a stool, sifting through an array of seed packets. Across the broad table she fanned them out, like a hand of solitaire, into separate little kingdoms: the early bloomers, the climbers, the perennials, the bulbs. In the candlelight, the kingdoms wavered.

"So Joe. Why the limp? What gives?"

"It ain't sympathy I'm looking for. That ain't what I come for."

"You're picking the wrong day for pie."

"I come for the baker."

"The hell you say. What would you do with a baker?"

"Defend her honor."

"With what?"

"My manhood."

She pictured herself in the spring air, in the hot sun, at the center of that burst of bloom. Deployed the bulbs another ten feet closer to the base of the porch. Freed up another patch of sunlight for the perennials. The paper, stiff with the print of azalea and pepper and the red of the radish, crackled in her hand. "I seen a man before. Never seen a manhood."

"It's about honor, woman. My honor."

"So now. So. I thought this was about my honor, but no. No. To defend my honor, it seems, you gotta muster a bigger, a better honor, right? Gotta bolster that mud fence with the sturdy oak of the honor of Joe?"

He limped over to the window where the moon waited. Noble the glow. A step. Two steps. There. Settled. Into a silhouette.

"That's quite a limp, Joe—jumping like that from leg to leg, one leg to the other."

"It's the war, woman."

"Hope it ain't contagious."

"Battle of the Marne."

"I seen the movie."

"You shoulda been there. We—"

"I can picture it now."

"We—"

"You and the boys in the back of the Nickelodeon, and skipping school, and attacking a packet of Cracker Jacks with them little marzipan hands of yours."

"No, no. We—"

"Pecker no bigger'n a button in the bole of them knickers. Peeping up at the screen—"

"I'm a veteran, Maggie. That ain't no way to honor—"

"There you go. There you go. Honor this. Honor that. Goddammit, Joe. Every damn dish, you serving up a side of honor."

"But it's honor that—"

"So gimme the recipe. What's it made of, this honor of yours?"

If he'd of had a medal, now. There's your answer. Grand. The thing about a medal—Joe thought about the medal, this potential medal of his, with a touch of pride—you leave it to others to whisper the word of glory. The medal got a voice of its own. A ham or a shoe or a spoon? Dumb. They are what they are. They got nothing to say. But a medal.

"Illuminate me, Joe."

It was an insult is what it was. How would she like it if he was to ask her to proclaim, out loud, what makes her a beauty? He made as if to leave. He'd been fixing to clap the hat on his head, give her a little tip of the visor, and stride out the door. Lifted his hand to—but then he remembered the weather. Reddened. As if it was owed an apology, the hat.

Over to the counter he strode, so's to have something to lean on.

"Honor's in the doing. It's in the deed."

"So that clown show up under the bridge. That Dual of the Titans. You got a explanation for that?"

From his shirt pocket he pulled a smoke—Old Gold. Not a cough in a carload. Struck a match. "I got nothing to say. My deeds do the talking for me." Joe pictured himself at the end of a bar. Dodge City. Cowboy Joe. The thumb a-tap-tap-tapping at the brass buckle with the inlay of ivory, stack of poker chips in the palm of the gun hand, the Stetson—still smokey with the dust of a thousand head of cattle—pitched up onto that set of antlers up top the barroom mirror.

Maggie broke out another pack of seeds. Summer seeds. For when the sun like a blowtorch brittles the grass and bubbles the sap in the tree. She laid them out beside the spring planting, shade to shade, sun to sun, season to season. She talked as she worked, without looking up, in a voice no bigger than a murmur.

"Lemme guess. In your head you got a picture of a person, a notion about a particular person. It's this picture you been chasing."

Down the length of the counter he launched a billow of smoke. "I never chase."

"Chasing after. Sniffing the air. On the hunt."

"You mean you," said Joe. "Chasing after you."

"That ain't what I'm saying."

"You flatter yourself, Maggie. What makes you think you're the onlyiest flower in the field?"

"Joe, Joe, Joe. We ain't even in the same field together. We ain't even on the same planet together. But just for the sake of argument, let's pluck at the ribbon of this little package you paper me in. So I'm a flower now."

"And not the only flower."

"But a flower."

Sweet the way she said it. Here we go. Here the bloom. Joe smiled.

"What do you do with a flower, Joe?"

Joe loosened. Leaned his head left, right, as if to peer round the green of a thicket to find the berry within. "You lean up over. You smell it. You pluck it."

"And what else?"

Not a man given to poetry, Joe. Tried to picture himself with a flower, jumbo flower, bud the size of a cabbage. You paw at the blossom with the heel of the hand. You poke at the bloom with the rubbery tip of your—"

"What good is a flower?" said Maggie. "What do you do with a flower?"

"You… I don't know. You—"

"You don't know. You think you know, but you don't know." She tidied the seeds. Squared up the ranks with the slim edge of the arm and the hand together, like a spatula. "You got a picture of a person – a pluckable, a sweet, a breath of air—but that ain't really a person. Not a real person."

"Real enough for me."

"An echo. It's an echo. I ain't the one you on the lookout for, Joe. The one you on the lookout for is Joe."

*   *   *   *

By the end of the week, Maggie was back in business. Sparrow did the chores and the heavy lifting while Maggie set to baking. It's not as if they waited for GB to return—he'd never made a vow one way or the other, and his trips were always a ramble, but now? It was different this time. He'd managed to occupy, if only for a moment, that province of the heart Maggie marked with the greeting Trespassers Will Be Prosecuted.

She swept the porch. Marveled at the twister of dust at the foot of the broom. Up onto the ruddy sun it sailed. It's not a color, really, when she thought about it, pink. Not a honest color. An edge in the direction of red is all. Blue sky, clover green, cinder black. Pink? The privates maybe. Snout of a pig, boutonniere with all the brio of a hothouse butterfly. No. So no. She decided she hated the color, she'd always hated the color. When the boys'd bring her tokens of love—the ribbon and the rouge and the hankie—she'd finger the wrapper, baby it open like a crucible of gunpowder. The ribbon? Oh—a tourniquet! The rouge. Pepto-Bismol, no? The hankie she'd ball, up into her fist, hammer the fist, wham, on the table. Thank God I got a blanket here, here in the hand, to warm me in the icy white of the winter.

*   *   *   *

By the time GB reappeared—two weeks later and not a word in the meantime—Maggie had already convinced herself that, whatever he had to offer, she'd be the one to pay the freight. Round about closing time he appeared. Jimmied the lock and – through the diner in a glide around the dark reef of the tables and the bristle of upended chairs—made his way into the kitchen. She pulled a pie-tin from out a cloud of suds. Gave it a shake. Into a bucket of rinse water flipped it. Without a word he waited. Up overhead, from out the rafters, rigged with a strand of baling wire (and upended so's to make a shade), a lotus bowl of carnival glass hovered. Tempered, is what it did, the bare of the bulb. Filled the air with a coppery glow. She took her sweet time. Wiped away the suds with the hem of her apron. From a pocket plucked a hankie. Mopped her brow. Hurry Maggie? To hell with that. Nobody hurries Maggie. Into the center of town she clattered, that first day, at the head of a cart she pulled herself. Raised her own chickens, gathered her own eggs, baked her own pies. Peddled them door to door, and at the train depot, and off the front porch of the shamble with a towel for a table and overhead a (beaten to a crisp like the hide of a buffalo) canvas top.

He looked up. In a glance he gathered in the whole of it—this vision of hers of a haven, here, inside, under the tin roof and the rough-cut timber of the high ceiling, under the haze of tobacco, steam of the grill, scent of the waffles and the bacon and the hint of pine from off the sap in the rafters, under the hub-bub of the boys and the clatter of breakfast and the banter—a haven. A home.

Maggie measured the moment. Felt the floorboards yield beneath his weight. When he finally stopped that side-to-side rocking, that boyish hurry to urge the earth along, she straightened her blouse, swept with a single gesture the hair from her eyes, and turned.

He unfurled the paper, bowed, and—without a word—laid it like a feather in her hand.

"So you take it upon yourself—" She held the deed up, at arm's length, like you hold a fish for a photo. He fingered the clasp of the tie that graced the red shirt he wore. Egyptian cotton, fresh from out the box, embossed with a set of creases quadrilateral and a stick-pin at the collar and, in a jig at the sleeve like a topwater popper, a yellow tag. Aratan Arrow, half-price.

"Take it upon yourself." She gave the deed a shake. "To come serving up a letter. Letter with a GB at the end."

"It's in honor of you. I did it for—"

She sang out the syllables: Geee… Beee. Onto the counter she pressed the deed. Bore down with the flat of her palm.

"And GB'd stand for what?" She began to buff the wood. The deed the buffer. "Good old boy? Governor B? God of the Beggers?"

Crackle of parchment. In trade with the townfolk, GB was the consummate grifter, but in matters of love? Maggie had always mocked him for his loyalty to her, told him the only thing worth a damn is the ground you stand on when you stand your ground, so he took her at her word. Dumb like a dog he believed her.

"GB the one to bless the bird and the beast and the crab in a scuttle at the bottom of the sea."

The paper curdled.

"GB the one to consecrate a quarter acre out of pity for the—" she wanted to say cripple but the word a bitter one— "the girl with the pie."

Stopped. Raw the palm. With the back of her hand she brushed away the fragments. "Such a fuss about a scrap of paper, GB. Shame on you."

"That's a carbon, Maggie. Got the original on file at the County Office."

"And nobody the wiser till you come along."

"I bought the land to keep it safe."

"Out from under me, right?"

"You talkin like it's a portable thing. It's land, Maggie. It's the earth."

"And now you got the deed."

"I got the deed on account a you."

"And what am I? A vagrant? A beggar for a crumb?"

"That ain't what I got it for. I got the deed—"

"Bully for you."

"—to keep it out the hands of the others."

"The last I heard it weren't nobody's."

"You heard it wrong. I did the digging. Got the deed

from the County Courthouse."

"So this piece of paper give you the right to—"

"It's a piece of paper is all. It don't mean nothing. Not between you and me."

"Then why'd you go digging? Why'd you bring it here?"

"It's a gift, Maggie. Ain't nobody ever offer you a gift?"

"I got the gift of sight, that's what I got, and what I see is a boy so taken with a tune he gotta turn a friend into a fiddle to play it."

"Nobody trying to play you, Maggie."

"You just gotta make a big show of it, don't you? You with the hat and the blazer. Pocket hankie. And the socks. Plaid? Tartan plaid? Goddamn ridiculous."

He reddened. At the oddest things he reddened, GB. Like a post he was, unbudgeable under the blow of an insult, game in the face of mockery, chipper in a battle of wits, but a off-hand comment about the cut of the blazer or the pitch of the derby, a whisper, a look, a wince in the wake of the aftershave and he burns. Go figure. Smack him with a hatchet he smiles: brush him with a feather he bleeds.

"But it ain't yours, Maggie. You don't own it."

"And you do."

"Until such a time as you got the means."

"To buy it from you."

"To take it on."

"From you. Buy it from you."

Not that it was ever her property to begin with. A squatter's what she was. But no matter. Maggie had always been a bender of words. To own. The only thing you ever own is what you take to be your own, she'd say, what you make your own, the earth you pierce with the banner in hand. She was the one furbished the room, tinned the roof, hauled a oven out the wreck of a barn to anchor it here, in the belly of the Feed and Seed. Built the kitchen around it. So no. To hell with the deed and the holder of the deed. The one with the claim was her.

Go figure, right? Even we—who fumble the kiss and paw like a bear at the door of love—could see what a match they woulda made. Pride. The very pride that gave her the punch, that extra bit of brass in the knuckle, kept her ever at a loss in the game of love.

Maggie the scrapper, right? You could fill a depot with the people who fought her. From the very day the polio struck, hobbled her in the sight of others, she set herself in opposition to any word of mercy, fashioned herself into a blade that severed the deed from the doer, that sheered away the whisper of love to leave, in its place, the cry of the broker.

Oh, you say. Cold. No. No, no—think again. It's not as if she hadn't been schooled in the ways of the flesh—the boys back of the mill in the season of bloom, the game of capture-the-flag you play across an acre of timber at twelve but—come the change, a summer later—up and down the slope of the skin. She gave as good as she got (this in the day before the polio struck) but even then the object of her pursuit—the lust and the fear and the wonder—was always the boy, the whole of him. Pride of possession.

Not so the boys. The boys a breed of their own. Say you take a flock of geese, separate the ganders, drive 'em (she read about this one) into a corral apart so's to ascertain the true object of their desire—the trigger, the taste, the sweet Dulcinea of the Secret Dream. Good luck with that. Turns out the trigger's a stick of wood the width of a triscuit. Got a single stripe of red. You fetch it up front of a gander, calibrate the height and—Geronimo—quick as them flippers of theirs can kick into gear, they set to humping the stick.

So goes the gander and the ape and the good old boy. Conflate the whole of a cosmos into a tick-mark. A button of bacon. A nipple.

So pride is what it was. That, and a lack of faith in the power of—no. Lack of faith in even the possibility of love.

Not that GB was any less prideful, no, but he was a practical man. Maggie laughed at the offer he made, as if it were a smallish thing, a parcel of air you append to a name—Mr. or Miss, Cap or Doc or Reverend—and not a piece of the very planet itself. No matter it cost him all he had. No never mind to her. She laughed.

What a sap he was, GB. A rational man, a virtue that made him, in the game of love—and we could all of us see it—a fool. He figured inches, feet, yards. Acreage he figured. The Slapjack too small a claim to carry the day. He pictured himself with a deed in hand to cover the whole of the earth, and the oceans to boot, and the grains of sand by the billion at the border between the two. Everywhere's where he would be. No place to plant a foot without a charge of trespass. Only then would he relent. Surprise her. Give her back, pressed down and running over, the whole of the world she'd—in her stubborn way—always refused before.

"Don't be so quick to judge," he said as he followed her out the back. She carried the rake. He carried the basket of table scraps for the chickens. "We make a good team."

"Not the word I would use."

"Partnership."

"I don't need no partner."

"True enough."

"I go it alone."

"But you ain't been alone. You been with me."

"With you? How do you figure I been with you?"

"Under the same roof."

"With the mice."

"Like a family then. Me and the mice."

"And the chiggers. And the roaches. And the cat, the tomcat scratching at the screen door."

"To keep you company. You should thank us. How lonely it would be without us kin."

"I got me all the company I need." The rake screeched across the stone floor of the coop. "Here. Right here."

"But now you got a bonus. You got me."

"And what the hell makes you think I'm in the market for a bonus?"

"You ain't never gonna find a better offer."

"So then I'm a charity case. That what you saying? You window-shopping at the rummage sale, is that it?"

"That ain't what I mean."

"For your information—and you can stick it in that dime store sombrero you wearing—you ain't the only offer I ever had."

"That ain't what I'm saying."

"Why just last week I got me a letter from a person of substance."

"A letter." Over the chopping block he leaned. Gave it a thump with the palm of his hand. "A letter ain't the same as a person here, here in the flesh."

"This particular fella been writing me now for a while."

"But you never seen him."

"I seen him alright. At the depot. At the train. I been around. You don't need to be tramping up and down the county with a map in hand and a carnation in the button-hole just to make a new acquaintance. And you with the—what do they call it?—after shave they call it. Like it ain't good enough, the shaving, like you gotta—splash-on they call it. Nowhere they say you apply it with a paintbrush."

"The only women I ever meet—"

"You got options. I know you got options. But I got options of my own."

The Spaniards got the feel of it. How it works. The Flamenco they call it. You got a fella and a girl in a swirl around a center invisible to the eye. In the center of the center is the place they're gonna meet. Or you think they're gonna meet. You can picture it. You can see them paint it, the possibility, in the way they move, the one to the other, like planets or comets in a loop-de-loop you thinking pow they collide but no, it's a miss. Round and round they go. What does it mean? In equal measure we near and we far. We flee the one we hunger to hold.

"So you got options. So this fella. You got a portrait? Cameo? Lock of hair? Tattoo?"

"He's a tall fella. Taller than you."

"Is he a dancer? This gal of mine, she's a dancer."

"Can't be much of a dancer if she dancing with you. You move like a mule."

"I got abilities you ain't never seen before. You'd be surprised."

"How come I never seen this gal of yours?"

"She don't live here."

"Don't ever come to visit?"

"Maybe she will. Just maybe she will."

So the game was on. Maggie pretending she got a fella. GB pretending he got a gal. They smiled like it was a joke. The joke a way to pretend. To play like the hand—that hand you reaching with—it ain't really a hand. The touch on the shoulder, it ain't really a touch. It's a stir is all, a touch of air, a breath without a word.

THE NIGHT SCORPION

by

LINDSEY HOSHAW

Chapter 1

The summer Wren's life imploded started out routine enough. On a Tuesday morning in early July, she scrambled out of the elevator onto the third floor of the Arizona Tribune newsroom, bumping into a cluster of chain-smoking reporters and sending M.J. flying—his coffee danced in the air. She touched his arm, mouthed 'sorry,' then weaved between the rows of desks stacked high with yellowing newspapers. Notes of vanilla and ash wafted off that morning's edition.

The journalists themselves were no less fragrant. Pummeled by another heat wave, they slouched in their chairs like sweating onions—their odor a constant reminder that Tucson was plunging into the depths of summer. Many kept portable fans on their desks or chalky sticks of deodorant in their filing cabinets. Others hung crisp collared shirts from their chairs for easy access as they shed another damp layer.

Wren made a beeline for Ben Greenlee's office. A wilted spider plant outside his door resembled straw stuck in a garbage disposal. A week ago, the leaves were perky and green. Each time Greenlee brought in a shrub at his wife's insistence, the neglected plant lasted less than a week before it languished and turned into the worst version of itself.

Wren knocked on Greenlee's open door.

"I'm busy," he called out.

Wren entered, holding out a single-page draft.

"No sign of his whereabouts and no updates from the police," Wren said.

As a no-nonsense editor, Greenlee had little patience for niceties. He made a grasping motion with his fingers.

"What version is this?"

"It's the fourth draft," she said, handing over the story. Greenlee leaned forward and scanned the article, his green eyes roving back and forth, line by line. Wren sat opposite him in a wobbly old leather chair with uneven legs. She suspected Greenlee never fixed them to keep reporters on their toes, literally and figuratively.

She was relieved she'd pinned him down. Greenlee prioritized meetings with senior editors and the Tribune's in-house counsel, Bill Rosenzweig, who fielded libel complaints and threatened competitors like the Phoenix Gazette when they ripped off the Tribune's reporting. Although Greenlee often acted like he was too busy for impromptu meetings, he never turned her away. She liked to think it was a testament to her verve and moxie. She'd barge in any day of the week if needed. Her motto within these walls was don't ask, just take.

She briefly turned from Greenlee toward the journalistic symphony happening in the newsroom. Keyboards clacked, the fax machine churned, and Richard Terry, the sports reporter, marveled at Wade Boggs' staggering .357 batting average. "The chicken man is on fire!" she heard Terry shout. Then it sounded like something toppled from his desk.

Greenlee cleared his throat and Wren turned her attention back to the draft between his hands.

"Porter is survived by his award-winning Shih Tzu?"

"Yeah…" Wren said.

"That seems gratuitous."

"The mayor took that thing to city council meetings."

Greenlee glanced at the jar of red pens on his desk and then back at the article. Don't do it, Wren thought. Please. I labored over that line. Greenlee paused, then handed the article back to her. Wren opened her mouth but thought better of it.

"Yes?" he asked, placing his hands on the desk.

"Greenlee, can I be frank?"

He didn't say anything but didn't protest either.

"I'm crushing these obits. I've turned them into an art form. We just printed the dying words of Arthur Jenkins after I spoke with his three-year-old granddaughter who he was pushing on the swing before he collapsed. Do you know how hard it is prying intel from a toddler?"

"And your point is?"

Greenlee removed his glasses and cleaned them with his shirt before placing them back on the bridge of his nose. His age belied his temperament. At 32, he comported himself like a septuagenarian. Aloof, terse, and restrained, he didn't mince words. If you fell out of his good graces, you'd have to claw your way back in—a process that could take months.

"Well…" Wren said. "I heard you're opening a spot on the City Desk—"

There was a knock on the door. Mr. Plaid stuck his head in. "You wanted to see me?"

Greenlee lifted up several stuffed folders, searching for something. After rummaging for a few seconds, he returned his gaze to Mr. Plaid. "Come back in twenty minutes."

He nodded and disappeared.

"The City Desk," Greenlee said and tented his fingers. "I didn't know you were interested in that."

"One thousand percent."

"You're interested in politics?"

"Investigative reporting." Wren plunged her hand into her backpack and produced a crisp piece of paper. "I put this together over the weekend." She handed him the cream-colored page.

Pushing his glasses higher on the bridge of his nose, he exhaled.

"Wren Stevens, Staff Obituary Writer," he read aloud.

"Everything is listed," she said.

"Part-time fact checker?"

"I check all of Eduardo's stories. Which, honestly, is a full-time job."

Greenlee held the paper closer. His nose twitched every few seconds. Was any of this registering? This whole situation made her nervous and sweaty in all the wrong spots. A familiar sensation took hold. Oh no. She tried to convince herself it wasn't happening but it was too late. The hives on her collarbone spread upward to her neck. She dug her nails in, desperately trying to alleviate the itching.

"What are you doing?"

"I'm sweating it out, Greenlee. Look at me, I'm suffering for my art." She could feel the bumps getting worse. She pulled her hands away. "Are you even considering this? I've got good ideas—who do you think discovered the measles outbreak at those elderly facilities?

"M.J.'s piece?"

"M.J.'s writing, M.J.'s voice, but it wasn't M.J.'s idea. Three weeks ago, I told him about those Silver Oaks residents being hospitalized, and boom, next thing you know—front page news. But I'm a team player, Greenlee. I never brought it up until now."

"Until it became a bargaining weapon."

"Weapon? I wouldn't say—wait, is it working?"

Greenlee removed his glasses and rubbed his temples.

"Give me the day, Stevens," he said. He took a swig of stale coffee from a chipped blue mug that said World's Greatest Uncle. "And tell Eduardo to fact check his own stories."

Wren stood up. "He said New Mexico was founded by the Vikings."

"He'll learn." Greenlee picked up the phone and started dialing. He pulled a red folder from underneath a stack of newspapers. "Give this to Paul."

As soon as Wren left, she realized how desperately she wanted the City Desk position. She wanted to be out on the streets in the middle of the action, not cooped up behind a desk writing about the deceased. She wanted to cultivate trusted sources that she could call any time of day or night to piece together the inner workings of Tucson's scandalous and corrupt city government. The situation with the mayor was more proof that something was not right in the Old Pueblo and she wanted to be the one to crack the case. She contemplated how to convince Greenlee of her latent talent as she went looking for Paul, aka Mr. Plaid.

On her first day at the Tribune, Wren honestly thought Paul's outfit was a joke. A rainbow of colors crisscrossed his pants and blazer as if he were an extra on the set of Willy Wonka. The next day, she walked past his desk as he draped another wild tartan blazer over the back of his chair. It was almost identical to the one he'd worn the previous day. This continued for weeks until Wren realized it wasn't a joke. Despite Paul's dizzying attire, he was one of the best reporters at the paper. He had a keen ear and listened between the lines when sources finally opened up. Wren sidled up to his desk feeling anxious and edgy after announcing her City Desk ambitions.

"Courtesy of Greenlee," Wren said, holding out the folder. He took it and placed it near a three-ring binder and a stapler shaped like Daffy Duck.

"That exchange looked important," Paul said.

"Do you convulse when you go in there?" she said, scratching her neck with her knuckles. The hives, those intolerable welts, were starting to subside.

"Nah, he's all bark."

"I can't escape the goddamn death desk."

"You've been trying for how long?"

"Two years."

"And you've been here?"

"Two years."

"Well, there's your problem."

"What?"

"Your ambition."

"What? Why?"

"You're chasing a mirage." Paul opened his bottom desk drawer to reveal a jumble of medals and awards. At least twenty medallions were tangled together. Many were tarnished and dusty. Wren thought about how long it would take her to win one of the Murrow or Press Club Awards, let alone ten or twelve. Paul was dogged, ruthless. Once he staked out a cartel drop-off point by hiding in a dumpster for two days. After Paul radioed the police, the lieutenant in charge dubbed him "The Midnight Trawler." He'd slowed down considerably since then on account of his age, his bones, the gout.

"It's never enough," he said. "There's always something more to chase."

Wren scooted onto the edge of Paul's desk. He cleared a few items out of her way—a dog-eared edition of Strunk and White, a pack of Big Red gum, a snow globe from the Grand Canyon, a paperback copy of Reagan's latest biography, and a half empty bottle of Pepto Bismol. Though she'd never admit it, Wren trusted Paul implicitly. In a room full of scandal-hungry breaking news reporters, Paul was an island unto himself. A loner of sorts. He'd been around the newsroom long enough to know when to react and when to sit back and let things unfurl of their own accord. He didn't see stories like diamonds and pearls. They weren't precious gems that needed to be hoarded. There were more noteworthy events than the staff could ever cover, which is why he happily took whatever assignments came his way and then used his journalistic skills to spin those stories into gold. It was his vision, his ability to pick out the nuggets that made him successful, not the stories or topics themselves. His wisdom had rubbed off on Wren. She'd become slightly more patient and realized every day the editorial winds shifted and you'd get another shot. She thought about this as she tugged at her hair and set her draft obit down on his desk. Paul read the first two grafs. He smiled.

"What? The dog?" she asked.

He nodded.

"It adds color," she said.

"Certainly does." He handed it back. "So you're looking for a scoop?"

"I'd settle for half a scoop."

"It's there," he said.

Wren looked down at the obituary.

"Where?"

"Read it again," he said.

She skimmed the draft. There were the facts everyone

knew—that Tucson's mayor, Elliot Porter, had vanished two weeks ago and was last seen inside his office at city hall. When he didn't return home that evening, his wife called the police. They searched Porter's office but found no sign of him. He'd simply vanished.

The police issued a missing persons bulletin, and wild speculation, errant guesses, and theories that couldn't be verified poured into the police department via the hotline number listed on the missing persons posters plastered around town. Several people claimed they'd seen the mayor at the post office, at the bank, at their Aunt Edna's 85th birthday party.

None of it could be verified. And none of this information was new. It'd been splashed all over the pages of the Tribune for weeks. Wren stared so hard at the draft she went cross-eyed. She shook her head and wracked her brain. She'd written this obituary in case Porter didn't turn up. But he could show up any day now. Maybe he was taking a vacation or renovating his winter home in Puerto Vallarta. Who knows? Anything was possible. She squinted at her own article as if it were a Magic Eye poster and something might leap off the page. What didn't she see?

"Last I checked the police didn't have any solid leads. And M.J. wrote an update last week including the tipline number. What else is there?"

"This is not a missing persons story, Wren. The mayor is dead," Paul said. He removed a piece of Big Red gum from the pack on his desk and slowly unwrapped it. "Think about it."

"I mean, there's a high probability he's deceased."

"One hundred percent probability," Paul said.

"Alright then, who did it?" Wren asked.

"That's the most obvious part," he said, and started folding the stick of gum in half and then folded it again.

"Enlighten me," Wren scooted toward him, nearly knocking the Reagan biography off the desk. Paul rolled his chair closer.

"Who do you know that is capable of making someone disappear and has more connections than God in this town?" He stuck the folded piece of gum onto his tongue.

Wren thought about this—there were definitely some shifty and powerful actors in Tucson. Mostly money-grubbing business tycoons. The crooked CEO of Lumina Energy, one of the largest employers in Tucson, had been arrested two months ago for siphoning money from the accounts payable department so he couldn't have done it. And Mayor Porter's arch nemesis—socialite Thomas Olfhander Jr.—had moved to Houston last year to reap the benefits of his family's petroleum fortune. With those oily millionaires gone, who else would want to take Porter out?

Wren bit her cheek so hard she drew blood. She touched her fingers inside her mouth, looked at the gooey mixture of saliva and blood, then wiped her fingertips on her jeans. Why was this stumping her? She searched Paul's face for a clue. His expression revealed nothing.

"If you want a scoop, that's your story," Paul said, screwing the cap back on the Pepto Bismol bottle. "Figure out who killed the mayor and you've got M.J.'s job. Shit, you've got my job. I could slide into an early retirement." He tossed the empty bottle into the garbage can. "Then maybe Rita would stop hounding me."

Wren took this in and felt the ground shifting. Something had opened up, a door where one hadn't existed before. If anyone was going to crack this case, they'd have to shapeshift. Uncovering the killer would take a degree of cunning she wondered if she had. She'd need to worm and charm her way into the suspect's good graces. But first, she'd have to find him.

A LEADING MAN

by

J.T. PRICE

America is Coming

"Rumor has it," said Jack Warner, cracking a goofy grin, halfway between amusement and bafflement, "the liquor industry is raising some fuss over your new picture, Janie. Odds are 50/50 Paramount never releases it."

Ronnie narrowed his eyes like a cowboy facing off with a distant threat, as Janie, visibly distressed, fluttered her hands over the tablecloth. The merriment of other guests filled their collective silence. The restaurant's owner, Michael Romanoff, threaded between his white jacketed wait-staff in a suit of his own, hair fastidiously parted, long moustache clinging to his upper lip and shaved everywhere above it.

"Apparently," Ann Warner said quietly, her green eyes alight with excitement, "they have offered Paramount millions for the negative. They want to pay Barney Balaban not to release the picture. It's almost like a backwards sort of poetry."

"Ain't that rich?" said Jack, juddering his filet mignon with steak knife and fork. "Imagine running a profit on all the films you don't release."

"Well," Janie said, "if they succeed at keeping *The Lost Weekend* out of theaters, I hope the liquor industry'll at the very least consider a pay-off in kind to me as well. I'll need the consolations booze has to offer."

Ronnie placed his hand over top of hers. Janie startled a moment, then withdrew from her husband's grasp. After some consideration, she moved her hand back over top of Ronnie's.

"I've seen some of the dailies," Ronnie said, "and let me just say, Janie's performance is terrific. It'll be a terrific picture, too. Really… ah, not a story to shy from making an audience question their beliefs."

"But does it make 'em laugh?" said Jack, forking another bite into his mouth. "Cuz if it doesn't make 'em laugh, I can think of time much better spent."

"It's a human story. The novel, I mean," said Ann, setting her silver-bangled wrist on the table. "About deep inner feelings."

"If there aren't jokes, no one'll care," said Jack. "Trust me, schnookums, I know of which I speak."

Ronnie raised his eyebrows. Of course a dash of humor never really hurt anybody, but a story about the intensity of a man's struggles and suffering, a fellow who longed to make something of lasting artistic worth but couldn't help getting in the way of himself, well—certainly if ever a subject merited seriousness, there was one. He lifted his napkin from the table and daubed at his mouth. Janie teased at her watercress salad. He brought another bite of chateaubriand to his tongue.

Quieted by Jack, Ann was now intent on freeing the wishbone from her en cocotte Souvaroff.

"We're here tonight among friends, aren't we?" Jack said. "Ain't that fantabulous—enjoying a meal like this among friends? You know, I can't get Ann out of the house for just anybody—"

Ann threw back her head. "Oh, if you're going to tell them that, then—"

"No, no, no, dear. I'm not tryin' to embarrass you. I only want them to recognize—"

"There really aren't many actors," Ann continued without batting an eyelash, "we'd call friends in the way that you two are our friends. There are, you know, a great many snakes in this town. People who smile at you one minute and sink their fangs in the next. Having acted on screen myself, I know a little bit about that."

"For me," Jack said, "the question is always who I can share a laugh with. I don't know what I'd do in the contrary. Ask my brother anything, and it's Yaweh this, Moses that. Serious as the grave. To me a good joke is the closest thing I know to god." Jack Warner set down his knife and fork and, tilting his head forward, directed a wolfish eye in his wife's direction. "Salvi Dally himself painted this beautiful lady, you know that?"

Janie nodded and glanced at Ronnie. Did she find it funny that their friend Jack Warner had apparently forgotten their presence at the unveiling?

"We were there, you know," Ronnie said. "At the unveiling."

"Ah, yes. Yes, of course, you were!"

Michael Romanoff had by then made his way to their booth. "Colonel Warner, everything was to your liking this evening?"

"Marvelous, per usual, my good prince. You see," Jack waved an arm around the table, then tapped the breast pocket on his suit jacket, "he recognizes my military rank even out of uniform."

"Why, certainly, Colonel Warner."

"Captain Reagan does enough representing of our boys in green for the bunch of us, don'tcha think?"

As Jack beamed at the table, Romanoff looked down his nose, then nodded and abruptly turned away. Noting the exit, Jack said, "All that mumbo-jumbo about Czarist Russian lineage? A lot of claptrap, he's no prince. The man's actual surname is… Gerguson." He paused, then broke out in a smile of genuine admiration. "Ain't that great?"

"Well," Ronnie said, "he runs a fine establishment."

"Certainly he does. We all agree. We're friends here, I know," Jack said. "Let me tell you then if I couldn't laugh when I see a picture, I don't know what I'd do. The whole world's got troubles. Even if, from my lips to God's ear, tomorrow morning we ride our tanks straight down the Fuhrer's throat. Then Hirohito on Friday…"

Ronnie found himself glancing at Romanoff's garishly decorative wallpaper as he processed Jack's blurring of sexual matters and war.

"But ain't all fun and tulips," the studio head continued. "We got radicals of our own, you see? And I don't mean Olivia de Havilland. I'm talking the workers, Herb Sorrell and his carpenter's union, this CSU. Rabble-rousers born and bred, they wanna strong-arm us into forking more dough their way? Ain't that great, ain't that peaches? Talk about snakes. I'm trying to run a profitable business, and this bunch are always tugging on my sleeve for a bigger piece of the steak. Well, ain't gonna work out that way. We got a man in the rival union we can work with IATSE. This fellow, he's someone we like. A friend. We'll work with him 'til CSU's all the way out the door and on the curb. Then see who's laughing."

Ronnie trimmed the fat from a piece of chateaubriand. Jack's ways were harsh, yes, but then given his role, perhaps he had to be. Sometimes, he just needed someone sensible to remind him what really mattered.

"My father always believed in the rights of organized labor," Ronnie said.

"And may he rest in peace, Ronnie," Jack said.

"Well, I happen to believe in a place for organized labor too. Why, can you imagine where this country would be if…"

Janie pursed her lips and scanned the room. She and Ann excused themselves to go powder their noses. There went her husband talking politics again. Or 'getting into it' as she would say to him with distaste. "We'll meet you outside," Jack called across the restaurant to the departing women.

He counted out the bills from a fold in his jacket with ostentation. "Well, now, Captain, would you say that settles the matter?"

Ronnie shot him a wry look: friendly, sure, but not in full agreement by any means. Let him settle the bill, but that didn't mean Ronnie had to accept Jack Warner's terms.

There was always room for a little productive jostling in any friendship. As they headed for the door, Jack stopped at table after table to say hello, grasping shoulders, laughing right into people's ears, as if he owned the joint, doting especially on a young starlet whose name Ronnie couldn't place. Once outside, Jack leaned close with a childish grin.

"I had her, you know."

"Pardon me?" said Ronnie.

"That gal in there. Twenty-two and already on her way to her first big role. I had her. Sweet piece of action."

Ronnie looked away, struggling to contain his scorn. Well, nobody would ever accuse Jack Warner of being a pious man. Or even a good one. In a way, that was what Ronnie liked about him. Even if he didn't like this particular facet of his character. Ronnie felt conscious all of a sudden of how much he counted on Janie, his own wife, for affirmation. It was a kind of vulnerability, in a way, his fidelity.

But she was worth it. They were worth it. Mermie too.

Now he looked again to Jack, as they waited on his limousine, and found that the studio head appeared to be offended. In his face was the boy from a Jewish ghetto who'd beaten the odds against him, every injury done. Would he be roped down by anything so quaint and genteel as the marriage concept, or decorum regarding so-called professional conduct? It wasn't Ronnie's defense of organized labor that had upset him, or his hidden scorn. Instead, it was the absence of Ronnie's vocal approval. Rather than admitting to a type of unseemly advantage-taking, it was as if Jack Warner had confessed a vulnerability for which Ronnie was meant to re-assure him.

"What are ya, Ronnie, a homo?"

Ronnie squared his jaw and looked down at the rank displayed on his uniform. "Janie'd be pretty surprised to hear that, I think."

"Only joshing ya, only joshing ya. But more than half of 'em in this town got wives, or hadn't ya heard?"

"Don't mean to disappoint you, Jack."

"Haha!"

"I only happen to be pretty well satisfied with the lady coming home with me tonight."

Ronnie then attempted a joke about the fake Russian prince and was saved, at last, by the reemergence of the women from Romanoff's.

"Girls," Jack said. "My lovely Ann! Let us, to our horse and chariot."

"Jack, dear," said Ann, arranging her stole, "if you insist on making a fool of me whenever we go out—"

"Ronnie and I were only talkin' baseball!"

"Don't go telling on yourself. Hanging over that girl in there."

Ronnie glanced from Ann to Jack, then at Janie. "I'm bound to agree with whatever he says. I believe it's in my contract."

"My husband," said Janie. "The politician."

— INTERSTITIAL —
THE BATTLE FOR WARNER BROTHERS

All that's happening, at first, is we're out with our signs, perfect marching order, about three hundred of our members and affiliated supporters, sweating it out for the cause. That big WB logo right over our heads. Now here come the county sheriffs shoulder-to-shoulder, in steel helmets and swinging nightsticks, driving us back. You know there's gonna be trouble because, guess what, they're wearing gas masks. I look up and on the roof above us, no exaggeration, snipers toting 30-30 Garrand rifles. How-de-do, top-of-the-morning to you! It's the war come home, but this time the enemy's working men and women.

The morning's October 5th. This was the Olive Street entrance, our seventh month strong. Scalding out there, sun's barely up, temperature climbing all week. Everyone's looking forward to the weekend. These guys got other ideas apparently.

All we're asking for is a better shake. We held off on striking all through the war just to get to the moment we're at now. With Roosevelt gone, who believed the Popular Front was gonna hold? We had to be ready for the tide to turn against labor. Had to get one step ahead. C'mon, I know these guys. Who wants to wreck their whole business for the sake of another Newport Beach vacation home instead of what we were asking?

We'd done such a number on Disney in 1941 that Uncle Walt came to the bargaining table in a snap this time around. Leaving only MGM, Columbia, Paramount, and yeah, the rest of the usual suspects. Including Warner Brothers.

Sure, we had some stars walk off the lot in support, and I won't forget it: Bette Davis, Harpo Marx, Joseph Cotten, Walter Huston.

They say Cary Grant himself skipped out on reshoots. Though, you ask me, Mr. Grant didn't feel like doing his reshoots, that's all.

Some of the real marquee names lined up with us too, under the sun, right on the pickets: Dalton Trumbo, John Howard Lawson, and Mr. John Garfield, a true champ, this guy. He goes over where we have our cafeteria set up outside the studio walls, steps behind the table, starts ladling out grub for our people. That's a stand-up guy, you see?

But the Screen Actors Guild, they refuse to take a side. They say, and—sure, I see the point—our CSU guys are skilled craftspeople, we can take other work while this strike goes on. We can build a house for anybody, they say. You know, anything except movie work. While movie actors, they're supposedly hitched to the business. They claim there's nothing else they know how to do. Their faces are their bread and butter, not anything they do with their hands.

I see the point but don't know how much I buy it. OK, let's say it's true. What I want them to tell me is this: How long you think the studio bosses last without their movie stars? How long? What, are they gonna make scab pictures starring Kary Grantt and Rozalind Rhussel, hope nobody notices?

No movie stars means no movies. No movies means no profits.

If SAG comes through for us, that ends it. It ends it!

Here's how the studios want it to end: a whole squad of Chicago goons with brass knuckles, six-inch pipes, hammers, and battery cables. This type, I know. This type, we were prepared to stand our ground against. But the police, who ought to be throwing in on our side, are in cahoots with the goons. So when a couple of cars accelerate into our people and the fighting starts, it's hardly a fight. We're getting blown over. I know my way around a boxing ring, I can dish it out to these bastards as good as I take, but the cops lob tear gas canisters at us and I got that rancid stuff all up in my eyes and my nose, my throat's closing, I'm stumbling around, can't hardly see, getting tenderized by thugs who knew enough to wear goggles and handkerchiefs around their mouths. It's right then the sheriffs turn the hoses on. Absolutely blasting our people, right up against the gate. They got us pinned to the outer wall of the studio.

I fall over and for a second I see it, the whole scene, as that spray blasts over my head. Sunhats turning end over end in the mist. They grab us from the asphalt and pass us over to sheriffs who throw us in their wagons. I know a supply chain when I see one.

"The Battle for Warner Brothers" the papers called it. An ugly thing. The public's offended. So much that the bosses have to settle with us, let CSU back into the working fold. "Nobody's victory," they said.

These bastards are waging a war. Don't believe me? Go, take a look at the record—it's IATSE and Brewer, our fellow laborers, in bed with the studios, and they'll do whatever it takes, any means necessary, to drown us.

'Communist' they call me.

'Un-American' they call me.

Now you got me here, telling you. What's that about?

They wanna make people think Herb Sorrell's a monster. It gets down to where if you do not agree with somebody, you must be a Communist. Rile 'em up, scare 'em nice and good.

I never met Joe Stalin. What's he hiding behind that moustache, I wonder? Quickest way I ever seen to make a Commie? Substandard wage scale. That's all it takes. I'm not being a wise-ass either. So give your thanks to Uncle Walt, not Russkie Joe.

I'm only a dumb painter, that's all. A dumb painter who had—pardon my being frank—the balls to stand up to Walt Disney. Next thing you know here come these bastards with their insinuations.

You see the ad they placed after we won our federal ruling in 1941? *"We are continuing our investigations of your leaders. We are not yet ready to disclose our identity or to* turn over our findings. *You must answer the question of your own conscience: 'AM I A LOYAL AMERICAN OR A LOYAL DUPE?'"*

Awful damn brave, don't ya think? Awful American? My dumb mug's splashed all across the papers—'Herb Sorrell' this, 'Herb Sorrell' that—and these bastards hug the shadows and stir their little cauldrons of fear. Speak up for fairer wages—all of a sudden they make you out to be the anti-Christ.

Tell me again, which side was Christ supposed to be on?

It's no secret: IATSE's mob-tied. Chicago-tied. Goes back to Capone. How do I know they operate like I say? Because they offered a bribe direct to me. Fifty-six thousand, nice little briefcase.

Guess where I told 'em to put it?

We offer a clean alternative with CSU. I run the show, so I'm in a position to know. We're by the book. With IATSE in the palm of their hand, the studio bosses got no plan to quit, trying to sway our brother and sister unionists against us. They want to push us out and give all our jobs to the union they know will make nice. These bastards encroach on our rightful jobs to this day, to this hour. Kick up jurisdictional issues wherever they can.

Any labor leader who accepts a bribe or a gratuity oughta be shot, and I'm not talking vigilantism either. A full-on firing squad, thirty to forty strong. Regular union members, regular folks, behind those rifles. Let's make it the law of the land. That money they're taking: it's a trade-in on the belief of every member, every due paid, that a union representative has his people's best interest at heart. It's Judas ten thousand times over. Not only are they betraying their members' hopes, they're replacing those hopes with cynicism and disbelief.

What's Roy Brewer have to say for IATSE? Take a guess. *The Conference of Studio Unions was born in destruction and it will die in destruction.*

And about anyone who speaks openly of IATSE corruption? *Do you, as an individual, support the campaign of slander, vilification, lies and scurrility now being carried on against these loyal American workers?*

What they're doing to us, they claim we're doing to them. Gotta say, I bet it read better in the original German.

You seen what they're doing to us out there?

You paying attention at all?

The name Herb Sorrell has been dragged in mud throughout these United States as a subversive element, and people who have known me all my life think something is wrong. They do not understand it. They cannot understand.

The people I'm fighting against have access to the press. They have a large staff of fancy publicists. They get their word out much better than I do.

Look, I make no bones about who I am. Yeah, when I was a kid starting at the studios I was prejudiced against foreigners because I was bothered by how they spoke. I was prejudiced against Jews because it always seemed like they had a hard time mixing with the group. I bought what I was told about Negroes too, I ate it right up, ignoring all of history, and the evidence right in front of my face. I'll even tell you I went to a meeting of the Ku Klux Klan. And you know what? Gotta say: I found their regimentation impressive. Even considered joining. But that was before I understood they wouldn't take Catholics.

Now, see? I had friends who are Catholic. And anyone who disrespects my friends is disrespecting me.

Over time I've gotten to know all different types of people. Visited their homes. Seen they were no different than you or me. Everybody working hard to carve out a place in this country. When I understood that, I said I'd do whatever I could to benefit working people, my friends.

I explain these things to you, because I want you to know that I ain't holding nothing back. If I was to join the Communist Party, I'd tell you. I got no reason to hide anything, especially that. Do I seem to you like someone scared to share what he thinks?

CSU has a place for everybody. It follows like night follows day that when you eliminate any small minority next it's gonna be a larger minority. If today it's the Communists, tomorrow it'll be the Jews. Then the Negroes. Then labor unions. Look, that was Hitler's plan, wasn't it?

Me? I wear who I am right on my sleeve. I got no hidden designs, no fancy pretensions.

I talk loud. I like a big sandwich for lunch and a long drive along the coast on the weekend. I like a great movie. *Grapes of Wrath*, ever seen it? How about *Juke Girl*? I love my wife and kids. I don't need more than one vacation home for my family. I have worked in a factory since I was twelve years old and seen direct with my own eyes what a strong union does for the workers. What I do, what my people do, it's vital to the finished product.

Lighting on a set is so intense it can eliminate all shadows, you know that?

To get shadows into a motion picture somebody needs to paint 'em there.

DAYTONA TEDDY RIGGS

by

DREW BUXTON

1

The dopey offensive tackle is shaking and has the yips. He can get it any way he wants. I got so many tools in my bag—swim, spin, rip, anything. I get down in a three-point stance and smile at him, but he won't look at me. The ball gets snapped, and I move my inside arm like I'm trying to hook him and get around the edge. His feet move sideways then I drive right into him—bullrush—and put him on his ass. I step over him, and I'm on the QB's blindside. He sees me at the last second, but it's too late, and I explode through him. The ball comes out. It's worth the risk of a flag when you're trying to knock the ball out and change the game. That's what Coach Gregory always said. That's what it means to be a playmaker.

I'm basically Charles Haley from the Cowboys. You can double-team him, throw three guys at him, but he's still gonna find a way to be disruptive. The only difference is he's playing on Sundays at Texas Stadium, and I'm down here in Corpus. Imagine the two of us together, one on each side.

The QB still hasn't gotten up, and everyone is crowding around him. He's athletic and has a good arm, but he's soft. I tell him to get up. He's in full pads, and I've just got on sweats and a t-shirt. Someone starts yelling Daytona from the other side of the field, and I don't even have to look to know it's Coach Juarez. I knew it wouldn't be long. He's had it out for me since seventh grade, since I first stepped onto this field. Then he tried sabotaging me with Coach Gregory at Tuloso. I know he told him I'm a bad kid.

Now Coach Juarez is saying he's calling the police, that he's not bluffing this time. He starts walking inside. He's probably not gonna call anyone, but it's not worth the risk. I tell him I'm leaving. I walk off the field and onto the sidewalk along the guardrail by the road that goes up to Granny's neighborhood, Cactus Basin. If Juarez was a man he would've done something about it himself instead of calling the cops. He's mad because he knows the kids really listen to me and respect me. They know he's just some old burnout. The game has passed him by. I walk past where the trees start and get out of sight. I can see them, but they can't see me. Juarez doesn't know. He doesn't know anything.

I could play in the NFL if I wanted to, but it's not my calling. The thing with football is you could be the best player God ever put on Earth, but if the man next to you doesn't do his job, you could still lose. The running back could fumble. The receiver could drop the ball. I don't wanna rely on anyone but myself.

He still hasn't gotten up, and I can't tell if he's moving because there's too many kids around him. Maybe it's what he needed. We need tests in life. Pat Dupree says life is constantly testing our commitment to what we say we want. How bad does he want to be a great QB? This might show him that the game isn't for him or it could light a fire under his ass to learn how to move up in the pocket, to grow eyes on the back of his head.

I can't worry about this now. I gotta get home and check on Granny. She could be dead on the recliner, just slipped away. She could've fallen and broken her hip. Stop, I say in my head. Stop. Stop. It's on me to stop the thoughts. Thoughts are real things, and they're energy you're putting into the universe. I counter them with thoughts of her smiling, moving around, being healthy. I start walking that way through the trees and start running when I get to the sidewalk. The gate ends where the trees start so anyone could get into the neighborhood if they really wanted. I gotta see her, and I keep these counter-thoughts running in my head. I gotta slow down for a second and walk. It's true I've had to sacrifice some stamina with the added muscle mass. Anyone who's serious about strongman has to. I walk as fast as I can. Only about three blocks.

There's sirens—Corpus Christi PD, and I gotta laugh. I guess Coach Juarez really did call this time. They're in the distance, but they sneak up on you quick. Everybody in the neighborhood has their backyard fenced in, but Marty, a few houses from us, never has a lock on his gate. I open the latch, go into his yard, and crouch in the corner behind this big cactus he has for some reason. He thinks it looks good. He's a hick from Beaumont who struck gold with oil, but he's still a hick. People don't just change when they get money, like when Granny married Granddad. She's still from Angleton.

The sirens get really loud, then stop. I hear their car doors open and close. They sent two cars at least. I listen for Granny to open the door, but then someone comes out on Marty's back porch. Goddamnit. Someone's home. I try to be totally still behind the cactus.

"You think I can't see you behind that cactus, you big son of a bitch?" It's Larry, Marty's son. He's fifteen or sixteen, and he's a little punk. "Come out," he says and pumps his shotgun. The kid is obsessed with guns, always going hunting and trying to shoot birds and squirrels in the neighborhood with his pellet gun.

I put my finger to my lips and point out front. "Cops," I say as quiet as I can, and he looks at me confused and motions with the gun for me to leave. I step out from behind the cactus and keep my head crouched so they can't see me poking out over the fences. It's hard to hide when you're 6'6".

"Go on," Larry says. I swear. If he didn't have that gun and Marty wasn't my buddy, I'd smack the hell out of him. He's one of these people that prays for someone to break into their house one day so they have an excuse to shoot somebody. I walk through the gate and move into our next door neighbor's side yard and creep along the house until I can just peek around the corner. A neighbor across the street comes out of her front door. Christ. I move back a little. People in Cactus Basin aren't used to the cops coming around. I stay glued to the side of the house and don't move an inch. She doesn't see me, and she gets bored and goes back inside.

I look around the corner again, and there's two cop cars.

I move up a little further and see all the way around. I can't see Granny, but I can see the officers talking to her through the door frame. She's okay. There's three cops. I recognize John Wells but not the other two. John knows Granny well, and he's the one talking.

She lets them inside, and I gotta stay put. I hear them go out into our backyard, and Granny's saying something about how I just miss playing football. John says, "Boy, could Daytona play." He was a junior when I was a freshman, I think. He wasn't much of a cornerback, but everybody loved him in the locker room.

They talk for a few more minutes about nothing then go back inside then back into the front yard. Granny says she'll tell me to go straight to the station when I get home. The car doors open and close, and I hug the side of the neighbor's house when they drive past. I wait a minute then go inside through the front door. Granny doesn't look up from the stove.

"I figured you were close by," she says.

"What'd they want?"

"They said you hurt some boy at the middle school," she says. "What the hell were you down there messing with them for?"

"I was just showing them some stuff," I say. "Coach Juarez needs help."

"I don't think he wants your help." She turns to me and pinches my arm. "You're too big a boy to be playing with those kids."

"I wouldn't be doing them any favors taking it easy on them."

"You don't need to be messing with them," she says again and looks me right in the eye. "You need to worry about yourself. You got too much time on your hands when you should be busy working."

They said the kid was hurt, and I start worrying it's bad. Maybe he couldn't move and they had to cart him off. He could be paralyzed or maybe his leg is broken.

"Did they say how bad he was hurt?"

She shakes her head. I could call the hospitals and check if he's in there. He's probably fine. Just got the wind knocked out of him.

Granny's right. It's not worth my time. Football isn't my game anymore. Strongman is.

2

I can't stop thinking about that kid lying there in the grass. Why'd I have to go through him like that? I could've just wrapped him and set him down. I don't sleep at all, and I decide to go down to the police station as soon as it opens in the morning and turn myself in. John Wells can tell me what happened, how he's doing. Granny is telling me to go too.

At 7am, I drive to downtown Corpus, and it's pretty much empty this time of the morning. People don't really start moving until eight or nine. I park on the street outside the station and put two quarters in the parking meter.

I go inside and the lady at the front desk says, "Daytona! Good morning." I forget her name, but everyone knows me here. Everyone in Corpus basically. I was all-county, the best player in South Texas.

"John Wells was just talking about you," she says.

I tell her that's who I'm looking for. "Did he say how the kid is doing?"

"No."

She tells me he's on his way and to take a seat. She asks if I'd like some coffee, but I say no thank you. I'm too goddamn restless already, and I just wish he'd show up.

I sit there bouncing my leg for 45 minutes before he comes in and he sticks his hand out to shake mine. "Daytona Teddy Riggs, come on back." It's a small station with the desks all in one big room, besides the captain, who's got his own office. John Wells sits in his desk chair and leans back and asks me how I've been doing. He's gonna ask me if I'm working, and I don't wanna talk about all that so I just get to it.

"I just wanted to see how that kid was doing. Granny told me to come see you." "Yeah, we came by. It was good seeing her. How's she doing?"

I tell him she's fine but what about the kid.

"Totally fine. Just got rattled a little there. Knocked the wind out of him I think. So what were you doing down there?"

I tell him I just wanted to help the kids and help out Coach, show them a few moves. "Well, I really don't think Coach Juarez wants your help."

I shake my head. "He needs all the help he can get."

"Sometimes I think you forget how goddamn big you are." He laughs. "I remember when y'all were in the district championship, '87 or '88 I think it was. Fourth down, the dude was open and the guy drops back. I thought Tuloso was done. Then out of nowhere here comes big ol' Daytona Teddy Riggs off the edge to get the sack. What was your forty, senior year?"

"4.5," I say.

"I still haven't seen a big dude move like that since. Not around here anyway."

I don't wanna waste time talking about football right

now. I look at him serious, bouncing my leg. "What now?"

"Okay," he says. "I'm not gonna lie to you. The kid's mom wasn't happy. She wanted to press charges, but I'll talk to her today. I'll tell her you just wanted to help and got a little carried away. I'll tell her I've known you for years and you're a good guy and that you won't be back."

"I'm really sorry," I say. I'm an idiot.

"I know you are, Teddy. I know you are. It'll be fine." He stands up, and I get up, and we shake hands. He puts his hand on my back as we're walking to the door and says I can't ever go back to the school again. Not ever again.

3

Granny thinks she's the reason I got off easy. She says she sweet talked them and that I better straighten out because what am I gonna do after she's gone. There's not gonna be anybody to bail me out.

"I hate when you start talking like that," I say. "It's like you wanna die or something."

"I don't wanna die. I'm just not scared of it since your granddad passed." He's been gone almost two years now. I wanna tell her how she's bringing herself closer to the grave with her energy, but it always starts a fight. Pat Dupree would say that if you think about dying all the time, you're gonna get hit by a car or something, but Granny says God's already decided what's gonna happen, and there's nothing that can change that.

She fixes me a dozen scrambled eggs, and I cover them with tomatillo sauce. You gotta switch it up and do different flavors and sauces on your eggs or you'll go nuts. Force feeding is the hardest part about being a strongman. Most people have no idea how hard it is to eat when you're not hungry.

Chewing and swallowing. Chewing and swallowing. Chew so much your jaws get sore. You're like a cow just grazing all day.

When she leaves the kitchen and sits down in her chair in the living room, I go out to the garage and get my kit from the fridge where she likes to put all her cokes, her caffeine-free Diet Cokes, and different stuff she gets for me. I keep my kit in my pencil box from elementary school all the way in the back behind all the cans. I don't know if she knows.

I go to my bedroom and do thirty or so milligrams of Deca anabolic in my ass and then my 100 milligrams of Diana. I like to do it after breakfast. If I wait too long after eating, it gives me a stomachache.

I go out to the backyard and take my shirt off. It's hot as hell outside—August in South Texas. People always whine about the heat on the coast, the humidity. You start sweating as soon as you step outside, but I love that. As soon as I step outside, I'm getting warmed up, getting my body hot and loose.

I've got a lot of equipment out here, so I don't have to go to the gym twice a day like before. I grab some light stones and do overhead presses. I grab a bigger stone and carry it back and forth, shield-carry style, hugging it against my chest. I do my visualizations. I've been telling the universe I'm gonna win Gulf's Strongest Man, and the universe has been responding. I said it for months, then they announced it's gonna be in Houston where the Pat Dupree seminar is gonna be the week before. It's all lined up for me. The seminar is what I spent the last of my trust payment on when my parents cut me off. Three thousand dollars, but it's gonna be worth every penny.

I work on frame carry. I built it out of wood and cast iron and attached door handles to hold on to. I'm not sure how much it weighs exactly, but I think somewhere around 550 lb. I want my own atlas stones to work with, but they're hard to find. Jorge had his custom made and shipped to Corpus, and I know it cost a fortune. He comes from old Texas money like I do. His family has been in oil for generations.

Riggs Gas, you see it on so many pickups. That's us. Started by Granddad's dad. People think I'm broke because I don't have much money right now, but they have no idea. It's just because of all this shit with my mom and dad. They said they can't support me doing what I'm doing. My dad wants me to come work with him, but that's not my destiny.

I pick up the biggest stones and get them onto my chest. You've gotta get off the ground then squat and hug the thing before you come up with it. These are easier than the atlas stones that'll be in the competition because they're not perfectly smooth and there's something to grab onto. They're okay for practice though. I pick up my biggest one I have and let out a big breath and walk from one side of the yard to the fence on the other end and drop it. It makes these little craters in the moist dirt.

4

There's a true story Pat Dupree likes to tell about a man named Joe who wanted more than anything to be successful in life. He didn't know how to become successful, so he found the most successful guy he knew, this guy Bob. Bob owned a bunch of real estate and restaurants and he had a big family, a beautiful wife and three beautiful children. Joe found him one day playing golf and asked how he became so successful, and Bob just laughed at him and told him to go away.

A few weeks go by then Joe saw Bob at a restaurant out with his family. Joe went up to him and apologized for interrupting but if he could just tell him one tip for success. Bob told him to leave him alone so he can enjoy dinner with his family.

Bob was discouraged but he wouldn't give up. He kept looking for Bob everywhere around their town, but he never ran into him again. Eventually, he said fuck it and just went right up to his front door. It was the big house on the hill. He knocked on the door, and Bob answered and tried to slam the door shut, but Joe stopped it with his foot.

"You're not gonna get rid of me," Joe said dead serious. Bob looked right back at him and stared him down.

"You really wanna be successful?" Bob said.

Joe nodded.

"Six a.m. Tomorrow. The courthouse. Be there," Bob said, then slammed the door for good this time. Joe couldn't believe it and yelled thank you through the door and said he'd be there.

He set three alarms so he wouldn't sleep in and put on his best suit. He got there early at 5:45, but Bob was already waiting for him.

"You ready to learn the secret?"

Joe said, "Yeah, of course. What is it?"

Bob started walking away and said to follow him. They walked for a while, and Joe asked if they were close to wherever they were going. He was wearing dress shoes, and his feet were killing him. Bob didn't answer him though. It was a coastal town, and they were getting close to the beach. It was humid and Joe was sweating in his suit.

They got to the beach and Joe demanded to know where they were going and said he wasn't walking in the sand in his nice shoes. Bob didn't even look back at him and kept walking. Joe took off his shoes and carried them and caught up with Bob standing with the water at his feet.

"We're going for a swim now?" Joe said as a joke, but Bob started walking into the water fully clothed. Joe didn't want to get his best suit wet, but he finally said fuck it and followed him. They got into knee-deep water and kept going until the water was at their necks and the waves were splashing over their heads.

"Are you ready for the secret?" Bob asked again, and Joe was like yes, for Christ's sake.

Suddenly, Bob grabbed the back of Joe's head and dunked it underwater. He held it there as Joe started to panic and kick and fight. Finally, Bob let him up and Joe gasped for air and was like what the hell was that for?

"When your head was underwater, what did you want to do?"

"Breathe," Joe said.

"Exactly," Bob said and started to swim back to shore. Joe didn't understand. He asked what Bob meant.

"How is that a secret for success?" he said.

Bob turned to him and said, "You'll be successful as soon as you want to succeed as bad as you wanted to breathe right then."

Joe got it right there. It's just about wanting it and fighting for it. There's a lot of strong guys out there, but I want it more than any of them.

Tonight I drive to the beach full of desire and intention, listening to the Unleash the Tiger Inside tape on the way. I like to go to the beach at night because it's mostly empty, and there's no one there to tell you not to drive on the sand. Pat is talking about how the only way you get certainty in life is by doing certainty every day. I don't think that I'm going to win World's Strongest Man. I don't hope I win. I know every day. The reason I know is because of the work I put in.

I get on Ocean Drive and open up the Chevy truck V8. I can't help it when I'm driving at night with the shore right next to me. You get drunk off that sea wind. There's nothing like summer nights in South Texas. I can't explain it. I hit 95 on a straightaway. Fastest on the field and fastest on the road: Daytona.

I slow down and turn onto Shoreline and into the Mc-Gee Beach parking lot. There's two cars there, probably teenagers who wanna smash in the sand. People do it all the time, and it's disgusting. The worst is people who wanna get caught. They'll do it in broad daylight.

I turn on the four-wheel drive and go over the curb onto the sand. It's brown and hard like wood chips, so it's easy to drive on. I drive away from the parking lot where I can get some coverage and you can't see it so easy from the road. I take out the Pat tape and put in Motley Crüe, Dr. Feelgood.

This is the real shit they don't play anymore. All the shit now like Pearl Jam is just whining pretending to be rock. Eddie Vedder goes I know you'll be a star in somebody else's sky, but why why why won't it be mine? Haha. If you actually listen to the lyrics it's corny as hell.

I put the Chevy in neutral and get the chain out of the bed and hook one end to the front hitch and the other to my sled harness. I put the harness on and tighten the straps. It's like one of those dog collars that goes on the whole body instead of just pulling on the neck. I take the smelling salts out of my pocket and take a whiff. Goddamn that wakes you up!

I jump up and down, and when "Rattlesnake Shake" comes on, I explode and bring the truck with me. It's all about how you start like a sprinter coming out of the blocks or just like how I'd go when the ball was snapped. I say I'm fucking unstoppable in my head over and over. That's what Pat says to himself when he goes on runs. I push forward, bear crawling through the sand, and my calves are on fire. At Gulf's Strongest Man, we're gonna pull a goddamn 18-wheeler, but it's on asphalt. Trust me, pulling a pickup on sand is even harder.

I pull until muscle failure. That's how you break through plateaus. I let out a primal scream and raise my arms. I'm at Oyster Creek Park. This was the last event. I got first in every single one. The winner automatically qualifies for Worlds. I see myself on that podium too.

TWILIGHT OF THE GODS

by

KURT BAUMEISTER

1
WICKED IMPULSES

A DOUBLE-STEEPLED, bronze-bricked Gothic at the cross of Warren and Dartmouth, Blessed Savior has been on that corner for more than a hundred years. Through world wars and great depressions, terror scares and countless recessions—through an American Century of money, blood, and long-forgotten love—Blessed Savior has been there. Or, rather, it's been here, hawking its wares, doing its do.

Spires climbing into the starlit dark, searching for whatever it is spires have always been searching for, the church has taken its age gracefully, façade barely betraying the slower, deeper decay, the architectural osteoporosis, lurking beneath its skin. Working that corner, rain or shine, snow or sleet, Blessed Savior has always reminded me a little of a pusher standing his beat, selling the lies he bought himself once upon a time.

You think that's wrong, right? Bad? Evil? But it's only logic. Because no matter how bad life gets, no matter the flaming slings and venomed arrows good old Fate pitches our way (more on that one in a minute), we cling to what we have, whatever that is. What Blessed Savior has is the Father,

Son, and Holy Ghost, even though none of them are real. And what I have is you, even though you don't think I exist.

I TAKE the steps two at a time. Sure, they're iced over, badly—this is winter in Boston—but that doesn't bother me, not really. I've still got talents, skills, bona fides, if you will. Not that I'd measure up to what you've learned to think of as a god. None of us would.

Between your jacked, spandex-packed comic book heroes barging across the silver screens and your sitcom gods clogging up the little ones, you've tricked yourselves into believing we can't possibly be real. We're creatures of blue screen, phantoms conjured from the narrative ether, nothing more. That's where you're wrong, though. We're not ghosts, not us. At this point we're very much flesh and blood, more like you than we've ever been. More like you than you could possibly imagine.

Take me. I've got no horned helm or black, flowing mane, no ever-present smirk or scheme-furrowed brow. I have dark black skin, a shaved head, and a friendly, trustworthy face. Truth is, I look a lot like a cross between a young Denzel and a young Taye Diggs. And, man, does it piss Odin off. No, not looking like a movie star. It's the black skin that gets him. Not that I can really take credit for it. Fate gave us new, static forms after Odin and the rest of them fell. Who knows why? I mean, that's the thing with Fate, isn't it? We never really know what she's up to until the Norns tell us, but the Norns are gone, have been for centuries.

Don't misunderstand me: It's not that I want or need you to care about me or how I look. Loki's here if you want him, and if you don't, you don't. Odin on the other hand… well, he's roiling, has been ever since…honestly, I can't remember a time when One-Eye hasn't been seething with miscast rage at all the "slights" you guys have laid at his sanctimonious boots. No, the All-Father is not your pal, no matter the snowscape wishes and fairytale dreams you feed yourselves time and again.

Hanging from a magic tree to bring wisdom to humanity? Enthroned in far Valhalla, granting boons to the most valorous of warriors? Magic spears and talking heads? Sorcerous ravens and preternatural wolves? Eight-legged horses? I mean, seriously…how did he come up with this stuff? Don't answer that. Please, don't. I know exactly how he came up with it because I helped him. And I'm sorry, little ones, oh, so sorry.

But isn't that what you'd expect of real evil? Not some pat, cartoon devil twirling his mustache and muttering a caustic "drat" every now and again, but an avatar of light, a pretense of good, honor, and nobility when the truth is the opposite, when Odin is the source of pain, both yours and mine. If he hadn't started meddling in your lives way back when, if he hadn't cast me out of Asgard time and time and time again, what a wonderful world it would be.

FRESHLY WAXED linoleum floors of pale spearmint -green and walls of saffron-yellow cinder block: Blessed

Savior's basement is an interior decorator's acid trip gone completely to shit. Shuddering fluorescents loom overhead, emitting a low-grade buzz as lonely motes circle the spindly silver bars suspending the lights from the ceiling. The lights remind me of bug traps at some backyard soiree waiting to go zippety-zap on uninvited guests. Heavy, floral perfumes and 100-proof colognes linger from the Council for American Purity meeting that broke an hour ago. I know those people, those CAPs. They're hell on two legs, Odin's own special angels. And they're everywhere these days. Yes, it's true, my dears: even in America.

Hooting about the taxes they don't pay, and the welfare other people shouldn't get, howling about their inalienable rights to Social Security, Medicare, and a white, Christian America. Something about being in the People's Republic of Taxachusetts, maybe, that makes the right wingers veer even farther right. That's how it is, though. That's how it's always been.

Back in the past, back in those last days of Valhalla, I always felt queasy when we were all together, like I was out of my element. And I was. I just didn't realize how bad Odin and the rest of them had gotten until Hitler came goose-stepping out of the grand old Weimar, a cancer of ego and animus, desperate for life.

See, what's true for you is true for us, too. Fate can still surprise us: It can still take the hope, love, and happiness we thought we'd found, ball it up and send it streaking into eternity's ever-ready abyss. Yes, we may be immortal, but Fate still rules our lives. Fate can still make us cry.

A PAPER cup of coffee in my left hand, a translucent-amber, plastic stir in my right, I watch the floes of undissolved creamer bob and weave across the caramel-colored whirlpool I've just raised to life. Forget about reality for a second—forget about everything you've ever known—and this cup of coffee could almost be magic. The way the liquid becomes a tiny vortex, the way it beckons eternal sleep, it's almost enough to make you, or me for that matter, dive right in…

I set down the stir, bring the cup to my lips and sip. Scalding, the coffee tastes like it always does at these basement shindigs, same as it did at the Gambler's Anonymous meeting I just left in Brookline. Burnt and flavorless at once—yes, it's a mystery even to me—Blessed Savior's coffee tastes of the irony implicit in repetition; it tastes a little like fascism to be honest, the fascism you keep buying even though you know you shouldn't.

"All right, Gustav, why don't you kick us off?" says our facilitator, Kurt, turning my way.

Kurt's my boy, my latest in a long line of human rec-lamation projects. Hair a dirty gold, slate-blue eyes, average height and build, good-looking in an unthreatening way (or maybe unthreatening-looking in a good way), once upon a time Kurt might have been the all-American boy. These days, he looks like a personification of various forms of privilege, though not enough to piss most people off. Like his looks, Kurt's vibe is chill. He goes along to get along.

In addition to running this unsanctioned Sexaholics Anonymous chapter—they all are, unsanctioned I mean—and his somewhat lackadaisical practice as a tax attorney, Kurt fancies himself a writer, a novelist in fact, a pursuit we share. Yeah, I've been at it a minute, since before Cervantes even. Man, have I got a few pages to drop on an agent someday.

Kurt's writing? Oh, it's not bad. Sure, he gets carried away with his prose and has a subconscious fear of plot, but it could be worse. Trust me, I've seen worse, centuries of it, not least from Don Miguel himself. You should have seen the fireplace fodder he penned on the way to Quixote.

Kurt's working on one of those serial-killer-thrillers these days, something he calls The Mists of Seeking. Minimalist prose, queer, female profiler as a protagonist, supernatural elements. His agent, Suzy-Sadie, swears "Mists" is going to be the commercial hit that has thus far eluded him. And maybe she's right. Though this isn't the first time Kurt's literary career has, at least according to him and Suzy-Sadie, been on the rise. One thing I'll say for the guy: He is prolific.

There was the satirical spy novel about religion. Suzy-Sadie shopped that to what seemed like every editor in Manhattan, from the ones she knew personally (not many) to those she followed or stalked or whatever they're calling it now on social media (lots more). Nothing. Next came the cozy mystery set in outer space and populated entirely by otters. That, too, Suzy-Sadie assiduously proffered to contacts, and non-tacts, near and far. Nada. Then there was the urban fantasy trilogy in which all the magic had to do with the ability to make fast food appear and disappear on command. No luck. The western, the contemporary relationship novel, the YA, the MG, the Harry Potter knockoff, the Goosebumps knockoff, the Lee Child knockoff, the parody about knockoffs, the farce about knocking off knockoffs, the pot-boiler, the spine-tingler, the tour-de-force-r, the catch-all, the be-all, the end-all, the catch as catch can all. Like I said: prolific.

Sure, the stuff gets published—most of it, eventually— though I wouldn't call Kurt famous by any stretch. That's the thing non-writers don't get. You can be successful—ok, comparatively successful—as a writer while making almost no money, maintaining a second career to pay your bills, and having no one know who the fuck you are. Funny, I know, but all too true.

No, Kurt has no idea who I am. That would spoil the fun, wouldn't it? But we have spoken about me on occasion. Dude practically gushes over "the Loki construct," tells me without a shred of irony how much he loves "the character," as he refers to me.

Imagine someone deploying earnestness when it comes to me. What a twist, right? Honestly, it's kind of embarrassing. I try to avoid the subject as much as possible, but he keeps bringing me up, says there's this novel about Norse mythology he's been meaning to write for years, decades even. I know, with that output you'd think there'd be nothing left in his poor little noodle. Apparently, there is.

"Happy to, Kurt. 'My name is Gustav, and I'm a sex addict,'" I offer with all the diffidence I can muster. See the down-turned gaze? See the batting lashes?

"Hello, Gustav," the group responds in a sort of echoey semi-synchronicity.

I cut my gaze as though about to divulge something so dark you'd have to stuff Secret Squirrel in a wood-chipper if he found out. "I had a situation this week."

"Yes?" ask various members, interest piqued. Others nod, smile, and/or avert their gazes. All I've learned, standard responses from Twelve-Steppers.

"I was at my dad's house, and I started having urges," I say.

"What brought on these urges as you call them?" Kurt asks.

"It was the Valks."

"What's that, a new dick pill?" asks a guy in a white Oxford. The sleeves of his once-immaculately-starched, now-immaculately-wrinkled shirt rolled up, jacket and tie dispensed with somewhere between the underlit anti-glamor of his corporate veal pen and the bright, Siberian chill of this basement, he looks vexed, distressed even. He looks like a politician surveying a disaster site he's about to get blamed for. "Like bicockatrix?"

Kurt cuts in, "No, no, no…Come on, gang, it's an indigenous tribe, like the Anangu. But from Europe." He nods to me for confirmation.

I don't correct Kurt even though he's wrong. How could

I? I'm the one who dished him this aboriginal fib a few weeks back.

"Valkyries?" he asked at the intake. "You mean like Norse mythology?"

I laughed, guffawed really, voice full of good humor and a touch of dismissiveness. "Naw, dude, totally different spelling. And we usually call them Valks. It's a lot easier. I mean, it sounds like a 'v' but it's more like an 'fsth' when you write it out."

"That doesn't—"

"In their language," I added authoritatively. "Trust me, Kurt-o, I'm only trying to make this as easy as possible."

He nodded and, of course, bought it. Yeah, I know I'm a Dickens, but what can I say? I may not be "evil" anymore, I may be good 24-7 (close at least), but I still have a few tricks up my sleeves. Fore- and first-most, I am one hell of a liar.

"Somewhere in the Carpathians," Kurt adds confidently. "No value judgments here, Gustav, but you've talked about these Valks before. Does it occur to you that this isn't just a simple indiscretion, that it's more like an abuse of power?"

"They don't work for me."

"They work for your father, though. You can't get around the fact that you're having sex with the household staff."

"What are they? Maids, cooks, charwomen?" asks the politician.

"Charwomen?"

He offers up his palms, tilts his gaze noncommittally.

"They're imported…I mean, guest workers, Einstein visas…Like I said, low cost of labor. Economic decision."

"You mean like slaves?"

"Slaves? God, no, they're like, they're… more like nannies," I add, smiling wide and white as punctuation.

"Nannies who get Einstein visas?" he asks.

"And you turn them out?" asks a woman with a buzz cut. Dressed in a red plaid shirt and a black, polythene vest, she looks like so many of you do these days. Woodsy and citified all at once, she looks as if she can't decide whether to hug a tree or blow one up.

"He's a pimp," says the politician, smiling, an understanding reached.

"No, I told you, I don't turn anyone out. I just had a threesome. If anyone's a pimp it's my stepfather. You should see how he treats them."

"Mm-hmm," he says skeptically, "Sounds like envy."

"Trouble dealing with authority," offers the woman.

"Control issues manifesting as wicked impulses," says Kurt, grouping the barrage of accusations into one manageable rhetorical missile.

A hush falls, as though Kurt's crossed a line, but the group can't decide which line he's crossed. What Kurt said doesn't bother me, mind you. How could it? He's responding to pure fabrication, mine at that. But it seems accusing a fellow groupie of something as base and Biblical as wickedness may have rubbed a few of us the wrong way. Which implies a fair amount of guilt circulating through our little gang.

Two beats without a sound and three and four, finally, the silence is broken by a woman's voice. "If you ask me, your father sounds like a freak, y'know?" The voice is smooth, light even, the tone matter of fact. 'Sounds' comes off as though it has a subscript z lurking within, like something from a German lullaby.

I turn to three o'clock and the voice's owner. A sun-blushed redhead with cheekbones that seem to go on for decades, she wears knee-high boots and jeans just this side of melodramatic. Long, straight hair, eyes of frosty midnight, honestly, she looks like a Valkyrie—a real one I mean, from back in the old days, not the invented version that has so recently run amok. And for the record, as far as I know, they haven't been around since we fell. Yeah, sure, I saw all of them eat concrete, that day in Berlin nearly a century ago. I didn't see any Valks, though, not one. Maybe that's why I make up silly stories about them. Maybe I miss Asgard and my once-beloved Valkyries more than I can even say.

That's not all of it with the redhead, though. I get this feeling looking at her, this feeling of progressive déjà vu, as though I've seen her before even though I'm sure I haven't. Yes, I realize that makes no sense. Still, I get this feeling.

"It's not like you forced them, right?" she continues.

"Of course not."

"So?"

"Exactly. Thank you."

"All right, all right," says Kurt, busting in. "That's a good start, Gustav. Sabrina, why don't we go with you next?"

"Sure," she says, surveying the crowd. "My name is Sabrina, and I'm a sex addict."

"Hi, Sabrina," they say.

"Hi, Sabrina," I whisper a second too late.

You wouldn't think I'd still be attracted to you guys after all these centuries, but there's just something about the human form, male and female both—the combination of energy and fragility, tragedy and optimism—that I can't get over; something about a pretty girl or boy, that can still turn my head and heart to mush. I'm smitten with you guys, it's true. And I always have been. This feels different, though; sends my mind spinning back, down a tunnel of deja vu: I don't know what it is about this woman, but it's something real, deep, and ancient, something that makes me think of the old days; of Asgard, Valhalla, and Fate. More specifically, Fate's servants. There were three of them them; three sisters named Sunshine, Halflight, and Darkness. We called them Norns.

"Why don't you give us a little backstory, Sabrina?" Kurt asks.

Sabrina replies, "Well, I used to be a therapist."

"Psychiatric?" asks the politician.

"Yeah, sure," Sabrina says, winking at me. "I had a whole gaggle of patients, practically an entire pantheon of personality disorders."

"What do you do now?" the politician asks.

"Not therapy, that's for sure."

"So—"

"Antiquities," she says.

"What?" he asks.

"I deal in mystical antiquities. Primitive totems with purported magical powers, stuff like that."

The politician opens his mouth, and I'm sure he's about to ask for examples when Kurt cuts him off.

"Okay, okay," Kurt says, "I think Sabrina's shared enough for the moment." He turns to the politician. "Let's go with you now, Percival."

The politician looks down, face tinting a bashful red.

"Have you done what we talked about last time, Percival," Kurt continues, "Y'know, forced yourself to stay out of the chipmunk costume for the entire week?"

"Well...," says the politician.

AFTER THE meeting breaks—after we sit through the sadly titillating tales of Percival the politician's shadow existence as a full-contact furry and Granda the bisexual exhibitionist's lapse as sandwich-middle in an unsuspecting deli's walk-in—I'm still surreptitiously checking out Sabrina, trying to figure out who she is and where I know her from. My other support groups, my various pro bono odds, and philanthropic ends... I scan my semi-fake life in my supposedly real mind, searching for the connection, looking for Sabrina. Nothing concrete, though, just that faint, lingering feeling of forgotten history lurking beyond reality's veil. Before I know it, though, Sabrina's up on me, electric, beautiful, and standing way too close. I can almost hear Sting's sandpaper contralto name-dropping Nabokov.

"Let's not play any games," she whispers.

"I'm sorry?"

"I need…" She slits her eyes insistently, scans the room, a spy at a meet making sure she hasn't been tailed.

"Yes?"

"I need…" More eye-slitting and side-glancing. More spy at meet-making-tail-check-ing.

"Yes?"

"I need to talk to you," she explains, without actually explaining.

I wonder then if I'm being catfished. I mean, it's happened to me a lot online, but never in RL. At least, not yet. Not that I'm making a value judgment. All I do is catfish people. Y'know, roam the world, making up and using fake identities.

The key difference between me and the standard catfish(er?) is I'm trying to help people. Always have, always will. But maybe someone else doesn't feel that way? Maybe someone thinks ol' Gustav done done 'em wrong and this is the beginning of some grisly campaign of payback? Maybe it's Odin even, wondering about me over there in New Valhalla, deep in the Black Forest? Maybe he's sent some minion of his to make a little trouble?

"Kurt's sponsoring you himself, isn't he?"

She glances at Kurt. He waves way too gregariously, like a five-year old trying to flag down Mommie at pickup. Oh, poor Kurt. He needs more help than I could possibly have imagined. I'm getting it done, though, don't worry. Kurt's my latest and greatest challenge, and I shall not fail him.

"Sure, but it's not about that."

"What?"

She brings one delicate hand to her mouth. "I know who you are," she whispers.

"Yeah, I know who you are, too, sis'. Don't worry. Outside these doors, mum's the word."

"I mean it, Trickster."

I grunt in subhuman double take. I remind myself of that misogynistic chimp-impersonator fro Suburban Monster. Honestly, it's embarrassing. I'm not sure how that guy has managed to spend his entire adult life making that chimp sound and making money at it, not just little money either, but heap big money.

"I have no idea what you're talking about."

"You still don't recognize me?"

"From a few minutes ago, of course.."

"It's me, Sunshine."

"As in Sunshine the…?"

"Norn? Right!"

"How come you look so different? Whither the cowled face and pervasive attendant shadows?"

"I'm different now. I guess we changed. We were gone a long time, y'know?"

"Oh, I remember begging you and those sisters of yours to stay. What was that, eight centuries ago?"

"I should have anticipated this reaction. Not about my looks, though."

I shrug.

"You've changed a bit yourself, Loki. I mean, you're black now, y'know? Or is this just a disguise?"

"No disguise. This is my new, static state."

She smiles.

"I'm still not saying I believe you, whatever your name is."

She frowns.

"For starters, how'd you recognize me if I don't look like I used to. Which I don't."

She frowns.

"For starters, how'd you recognize me if I don't look like I used to. Which I don't."

"I'd know you anywhere, Loki. I'm surprised you didn't recognize me. I should probably be hurt."

"But how?"

"Your eyes."

"My last form's eyes were blue."

"Not the color. The energy."

"Are you sure you're not just some actress Odin's putting up to this?"

"Of course not. How can I prove it?"

"I really don't know. Give me a little while to check you out."

"Check me out? You've been checking me out for the last hour."

"You know what I mean."

"Oh, the giants, right? And Hel? Still running around

with them?"

"They're my family."

"A pretty sordid lot if you ask me."

"They've changed, too. Just like me. And, supposedly, you."

"I'll give you twenty-four hours, but that's it."

"What if I say that's not enough time?"

She reaches for my wrist, grabs it tightly, and I feel something like a shock of electricity as she looks me in the eye. Yes, they're blue now, but somewhere, somehow, I can see the black gaze Sunshine used to have. Is this proof? No, it's not proof. But it's enough to freak me the fuck out, that's for sure.

I reply, "There's an Irish bar called McMurtry's a couple blocks back on Boylston."

"You mean the one you go to just about every night?"

"Have you been following me?"

"You go to a lot of support groups, don't you?"

I squint. "I'm trying to help people."

"And that writing workshop. What's the story with that?" she chuckles at her own pun.

"I'm helping them, too."

She slides her gaze down and to the left, as though she doesn't believe me.

"Really, this has been very encouraging. It's obvious you've already investigated me. We'll see how you like it."

"I'll meet you at McMurtry's day after tomorrow, ten p.m."

I leave ahead of Sabrina/Sunshine, then linger outside, blending into the shadows. A few minutes later I watch Kurt and her leave together. Never mind the Norn or un-Norn of it all, I'm beginning to wonder whether I can trust Kurt, my supposed buddy, fellow writer, and Sexaholics Anonymous shepherd.

THE LIGHTNING
PEOPLE PLAY

by

TIM CUMMINGS

THE LIGHTNING PEOPLE

My little brother Baxter sees things he calls 'the lightning people', but he will not tell me who or what they are. It's driving me up a rat pole. I don't even know what a rat pole is. I think I saw it in a dream, or maybe one of Bax's video games? But, it sounds like something that I, Kirby Daniel Renton the 1st, would be driven up.

About a month ago, Pop abandoned us and disappeared.

Dad asks me not to say that. "It's not true," he says. "We've separated for now, and he's in Texas with Granbuela, and that's all there is to it."

Yeah, but still, I tell him.

"Don't 'but still' me," he says. "There is no 'but still'."

Yeah, but still.

After Pop abandoned us and disappeared, Bax started having seizures, usually in the middle of the night. The darkest part of the night, that's when they happen, that's when he sees things. Monsters, or aliens, or people, or witches—I don't know exactly—who slink down from the lightning in a dark purple sky full of puffed-up clouds.

He says they show him things.

"What things?" I ask him, and get all fidgety, probably

from nerves. "Tell me."

But he refuses. "They're not yours," he says. "They're mine." He wants to keep them to himself. He'll be eleven in a few months. He one-ups everything constantly. The other morning, I got more marshmallows than him in my bowl of Lucky Charms. He tossed his spoon across the kitchen island and stormed off.

I want to know about the lightning people because I kinda have this thing with my brains. Dad calls it my 'magic', but I've heard others, like my teachers, say it might be 'mild OCD', or 'symmetry OCD. OCD is obsessive compulsive disorder, a lot of 's' sounds, like a snake is about to uncoil and bite you in the face and suck out your face juices. But, it actually means you like to be orderly. Or at least that's what it means for me. For some people, in severe cases, it's pretty high-key, as in buying 250 toothbrushes and throwing them out after using them for a milli-second because germs get on them so they can't use them anymore. A milli-second. We saw the doctor about this, years ago. But, I am not diagnosed. He told us that if it was not impeding on my day-to-day life in a negative way, then not to worry. It could be OCD, or something else, or a million other things. Or it could just be me.

I organize stuff. Not just books and boxes and junk drawers. It includes people, and feelings, too. I see people's feelings, as if they were colors, and I want to organize them. Feelings look like colored pencils that need to be put next to each other in the right way in the colored pencil box. When I see colors, I move them around. No one really knows about this stuff. No, I mean, my best friends Rockford and Ellie know, but they're all, "Whatevz, we love you." And Thaddeus Krasinski—he heads up YOUTHEATRE, our theatre club at Weirville Junior High. And yes, we call it 'youth eater' all the time. ('Theatre' is the act itself while 'theater' is the space where it happens. Krasinski is particular about that 're' versus 'er' thing.) He knows about my brains 'cause I told him after I rearranged the plays and books on the shelves in his office. Beige Blue Green Orange Purple Red White Yellow. Alphabetical by color. Colorbetical.

I need to know the lightning people are not going to hurt my brother, but it's hard to figure out 'cause I can't go up inside his brains while he's having a seizure. Doctor-of-Brains (the Neurologist dude) told us that the electrical pathways in the brain get mixed up for epileptics—that's the condition that causes seizures. Epilepsy. Bax was placed inside a monster X-ray machine that looked like a giant robot butthole so Doctor-of-Brains could figure out what was going on. He said Bax was an anomaly for being able to remember anything that happened during a seizure. He said that was not normal at all. Usually, people go unconscious. All I wanted to know, and all I kept asking, was, Why? How could this all just happen? What is it? Where did it come from? Why did it pick Bax? Stuff doesn't just happen. But the doctor said, "Well, yeah, actually, it does."

So, I told Dad my theory: that it's his fault Pop left. Hear me out: Pop is Bax's favorite person in the whole world, and the fact he could leave us—leave Bax—is what made his brains explode inside his head and that's what's cumming the seizures. After I told Dad this very wise theory of mine, that it was all his fault, he grounded me for the summer. Okay, a few weeks, maybe three, but it felt like the entire summer, 'cause during summer, when you're free, every day's a huge day. To have twenty-one of them robbed from you—for telling the truth— it may as well have been all seventy-five. Drove me up the rat pole, I swear.

And now Bax is changing. I see it. He's growing younger.

Bax has always been the smartest kid in any class. He likes to dress like a professor. Dad and Pop would buy him suits and nice shoes to wear to school. He doesn't like to look like other kids. He likes to look like Charles Xavier from X-Men. Always put together. Even though he's a little maniac and plays football and freeze-tag during recess. In the suits. We are used to this, how dirty he is when he comes home, so we don't worry. Other people think he's lit: the nice ties and big expressive eyes and shock of hair combed nicely with pomade. But, ever since Pop abandoned us and disappeared, and Bax's seizures started, he now wants to look like a stick of Fruit Stripe gum. He wears T-shirts with colored stripes on them, bright sneakers, and his hair is a mess. He looks… normal. But, if this is normal, it's the weirdest normal ever. And the real question, anyway, is: How do I get him to tell me about the lightning people? I need to know who they are and what they want.

Here's the thing: I won't let anything bad happen to Bax.

FREAK CITY

It's the Weirville Carnival tonight, best thing to happen all year. Rides, games, a giant labyrinth like in that scary movie with the maniac writer guy in the snow at the haunted hotel chasing his son with an axe. Except this labyrinth is normal. I think. Cotton candy, hot dogs, lemon-ices at the sock-puppet show. Motorcycle brigades. I could own a carnival someday. Maybe I'll fill my carnival with tall rat poles all in a row. I don't know. Something weird.

Tonight, YOUTHEATRE is raising money for the fall play. We don't know which one we'll do yet, it's still being decided, but last year we did *The Curious Incident of the Dog in the Night-Time*, a play about autism. I played the lead role and won this big acting award. When I accepted the award, I laughed, even though the Mayor of Weirville and the Principal of my school gave me the award at this fancy awards ceremony. I said, "Why am I winning an award? It's playing— why do people win awards for this?" It was a big deal for the adults. And Dad and Pop went nuts. Pop picked me up and spun me like I was a five-year-old on the playground.

Tonight, we'll do some scenes and songs on a stage off the thoroughfare. But *before* that, we will arrive early and ride rides and mash hot salty cheese into our faces. I might accidentally puke on someone's head down below while I'm hurtling above them on a ride, screaming my head off.

The Carnival down at Kerryville Grange takes place every year during the last week of August. Kerryville sits at the bottom of a valley and driving past Downtown Weirville, which we call DoWe, and into the open spaces is EEM. (Dad: "What does EEM mean?" Me: "'Enjoy every moment.' Keep up, Dad.") As you approach the valley from above, you can see everything down below. It's one of my favorite parts of the carnival, seeing it glowing and flickering in the distance while the sun sets all dark-blue, orange-pink, and purple-gray. The Ferris Wheel rises up, blinking its lights. I lean out the window to take pix with my phone and Dad yells at me not to fall out of the car and get splattered all over the street, and we laugh. I smell cotton candy, hot pretzels, hay. Also, the smell of a dead skunk on the road, what a funky stink. I hear old-fashioned carnival music. I think it's called calliope. It sounds all warped as it rides the wind, almost like a scary movie.

As we head down toward the carnival, Bax sticks his head out the other window and screams 'cause he's so excited. I smile, my face tingling. I can't wait to go on the Zipper ride that throws you up, down, over, to the side, backwards, forwards, spinning, lurching, jerking until you yack chunks all over. I hope I don't fall out and tumble down and crack my head open, but if I do, I hope hot pretzel cheese oozes out instead of blood. EEM.

After we arrive, we bolt straight to the ride, but the line is too long. We look up and see the machine, a big metallic colored centipede, its P-shaped carriages flipping around as the spine of the ride spins in a wide circle. Everyone is screaming. "Shake It Off" blasts from the speakers. The two girls in front of us are Swifties, never missing a beat, lightning on their feet. I tell Bax to wait, sprint to the front of the line to see if anyone we know is up there. Hoping to see Ellie and Rockford. Nope. Rats.

While dashing all the way back to Bax, to our place in line, I turn my head and see an entire stretch of carnival taken over by some buildings that say F R E A K C I T Y across the top in bright red letters. I stop, staring at it. I have never seen this attraction here before. It looks like its own little town. There is *Mirror Maze Way*, in a building with a giant mirror for the front, reflecting everything that moves. Beside that stands *Dunk Tank Drive*, and you can see through the glass of that building to all the dunk tanks lined up in a row. The little rooms are flooded with red light, and the dunk tanks themselves are painted with spirals, and thorns, and evil-long clown faces. Next there's a ride called *Freekout*. It looks like the gigantic hand of the devil holding four huge seating machines. It lifts them, rocks them, spins them, and flings them back and forth. It keeps moving up, up, up toward the sky, then it drops back down. I think I see vomit chunks flying out of it up near the top and I'm not kidding. Flying yackchunks.

Last in the row of buildings and rides is *Haunted Estates*. It is a purple and orange mansion, very Halloweenlooking. A mini train-track for the carriages runs out front. The carriages, with bat wings painted on the sides, take you in the house through double doors inside a giant witch's mouth. She opens her huge jaws right as the carriage is about to go through, and she cackles. The little car disappears, and the doors go THWACK THWACK with a loud crack of thunder. This looks scary. I'm definitely riding this.

I hop back to Bax, grab him. "Zipper's too long of a wait. Come see this FREAKCITY." I take his hand for some reason, the way I did when we were little kids, and at first, he's okay with it as he shoves pale blue cotton candy into his face. But after a minute, looking around at the teenagers and the carnival ride operators in their leather jackets and thick mustaches, he yanks his hand free. I tap him on the back, just letting him know how much I love him, even though he gets annoyed by that.

Suddenly I feel a hard SHWAT on the back of my head. It hurts. I whirl around to find DeSean Riggs and Jeremy Jameson smirking at us. DeSean holds a bag of popcorn, all greasy, which is what he used to whack me. They're 10th graders.

"Heard one of your dads split," DeSean says.

"Flattened by the Pride float?" Jeremy says.

"Splattered in the street where they belong," DeSean says as they skulk past.

I swallow, anger boiling all the water in my body. Bax's cheeks flood blood red and he lunges after them, but I stop him and place my hand on his chest to calm him down. Sometimes I think that some of the people who live in Weirville belong back in Texas. That's where we moved here from.

Dad and Pop didn't want to leave Texas. They met there, got married after five years, and used a surrogate for me and Bax. But some of our neighbors made life difficult. One day, we arrived home after soccer practice to find neighbors on our lawn with shotguns screaming Bible verses and Devil curses. Pop confronted them, and Dad shoved us back in the car and drove like 90 mph to the police station. I felt so scared Pop was gonna get shot. Bax screamed in the backseat the whole way.

We considered moving to Austin, but Pop said it was too pretentious. I think that's the word he used. Los Angeles was too far; Pop wanted to stay close to our Granbuela. New York, too expensive. Vermont was a possibility until we visited in winter. Then came an opening in Weirville, America's 'beloved rookie city' northwest of Pittsburgh and southeast of Cleveland, on the border of Pennsylvania and Ohio—but no one could move there because it had, like, filled up. No houses available. No new building happening for a little while.

But then a house came on the market, a dark-blue Craftsman, which both my dads wanted, really badly. After some finagling, we got it, moved here, and we love it. Weirville is 'America's freshest city, impeccably curated and designed, an imagined *Subtropolis* for the 21st Century.' That's on a plaque at school, and on the bridge downtown, too. It's on every landmark here. My dads say Weirville, as it turns out, isn't that innovative, not that different from other American cities. "America will always be America," they say. Pop says he never knows what decade we're in here. "Weirville is out of time—no one knows if it's the 80s, 90s, 00s, or 10s. It's an era-blender." I think it's a cool place to live. Except for crap-traps like DeSean and Jeremy, who make it stink here like the squashed skunk we smelled on the street.

I pat Bax's chest to make sure he has chilled out and turn his body around so that he's looking directly at FREAKCITY. "Whoa," he says. "A haunted house ride! Let's go!" He bolts for the ride, flies up the steps, flashes his neon bracelet at the conductor, and nearly slams into the people in line in front of him. The cotton candy has had its way with him.

The Haunted Estates ride has a long wait, too. I mean, I think there's only two or three carriages that go through it, and only two at a time in a carriage, and it must be huge inside there because it takes so long for them to come back out. Dad's waiting across the thoroughfare with some friends, sitting on bales of hay, eating street corn, corn dogs, and burgers. I only recognize one of his friends: the guy who looks like Ant Man. His dog peed all over our house at Dad's birthday party last year. They're sitting close to one another, I see that, and a fizz zizzles through my chest. I sigh, but it's more like a hiss. I miss Pop. A lot.

Bax's sugar crash makes him fall forward into me with a groan. I wrap my hands around his little head and give him a shake. Grgrgrgrgrgrgrgrgrgr, and he laughs out loud.

"Love you, Kirbz," he says. I grin.

Then he farts.

I shake my head.

"Oh. Look," he says, and points.

I turn my head and see painted creepiness: bats, ghosts, ghouls on the long wall of the front of the ride. Purple witches dance with black cats around a giant totem pole of lightning.

"That's like my dreams," he says all slow and quiet.

I feel twitchy in my belly, like weird little spasms. I swallow. "Your dreams?"

"You know," he says, "My see-thingies."

"See-thingies? You mean seizures?"

"Mmm."

"You think they're dreams?"

He looks away.

Looking at the witches, I shudder. They look so mean. I say, "So, are those witches like the lightning people?" I regret it, waiting for him to kick me in the wiener for even asking.

Instead, he yawns, "No, but I've seen them do that," pointing to their dancing. "But, it's different. They're not really dancing. They're just...."

I wait. "What," I say. "You can tell me."

"Shut up."

"Okay," I say, and turn away, feeling little kicks in my belly as if I am carrying a baby witch in there.

After a minute, he says, "They show me things, that's all, okay?"

"That's so cool. What things?" A million questions run through my head, a million possibilities of what they might be showing him. The secrets of the universe? The existence of

God, or ghosts, or Santa Claus?

"Things. Um. Symbols."

A shiver chills my spine. *Symbols?*

"What do they look like?" I ask, but as nonchalantly as I possibly can (even though I'm freaking out that he's actually finally telling me). "The lightning people. Are they, like, human?"

He shrugs. "They're outlines."

"Hmm?"

"Sillyheads. Uh. How do you say it?"

"Sillyheads?" I see aliens suddenly, the way some of them have gigantic heads.

"Sillyheads. When light comes from behind and makes an outline."

"Silhouettes!"

"Oh. Sillyheads is way better."

I cannot believe he is talking about it right now. What changed? Maybe we need to go to more carnivals? Was it the *sugar?* I wait, my head buzzing, needing to know more, but he doesn't say anything else. We shuffle up to the front of the line and the conductor goes, "Heh heh. You boys are in for a real treat." Why do they all have mustaches? Is it required that you have one, and tattoos, and a leather vest, to operate rides? He says the ride is brand spankin' new, created by designers who worked for Disneyland, so the effects are aces and the ride is super scary. Cool. Go, Weirville.

A carriage pulls up beside us, and the conductor gestures to the little gate, which opens so we can hop in. Bax sits on the right, and I take the left. I smell tropical bubble-gum and a sweet perfume, the kind all the girls in 8th grade wear, like fruity chemicals. The lights overhead dim and we're about to go in. I turn to Bax and say, "You can tell me anytime, okay? I promise I won't say anything. If you don't want me to. About the see—thingies and sillyheads."

But he's too excited now and doesn't care, clapping his hands excitedly. I join in, pumping my fists. A breeze that smells like salt and sugar ruffles my hair and face. The carriage lurches forward. Right as we're about to get sucked through the doors, a sign lights up in creepy orange letters:

NO SMOKING. NO VAPING.
NO LIGHTERS OR MATCHES.
LEAVE YOUR PHONE IN YOUR POCKET,
IF IT FALLS, WE CAN'T RETRIEVE IT.
KEEP YOUR HANDS INSIDE THE CART.

WARNING: THIS RIDE HAS—
JERKY MOVEMENTS,
CLOUDS OF HAZE,
LOUD NOISES,
STROBE LIGHTS.

Wait—did Doctor-of-Brains say that flashing lights are bad for Bax and could set off a seizure? But how many? How does it work? And how many strobes will there be on this ride? "WAIT," I yell, turning around and waving to the conductor. "Let us off!" Bax swats my arm, like, 'What are you doing? Stop.' The conductor doesn't see me though, and can't hear me either, because the witch's mouth opens to let us in. She cackles, and the crack of thunder is so loud, our faces vibrate. As soon as the doors close behind us, it's pitch black and all I hear is the sound of water dripping, echoing through the space.

"Bax," I say, "You can't look at strobe lights."

"What?" he says.

"If flashing lights come on, you have to cover your eyes."

"Why? Just shut up."

Strobe lights flash. Hundreds of them. They light up an old-fashioned drawing room or something, as if we're in Buckingham Palace. The room is filled with royal reds and golds and dead queens and princes and kings and their Spaniels sitting on velvety couches and fancy furniture. Cobwebs crisscross the space, the strobes flickering maniacally through the threads. I immediately clap my hands over Bax's eyes, but he claws them away.

A sign lights up: THE ROYAL DEAD, and we hear people laughing, people who sound very rich or something. Snooty laughter. The carriage lurches left suddenly, and another set of doors opens. Kitchen doors, the kind that swing in and out, and we move through the space, which is brightly lit so you can see all the pots and pans and spoons and dishes and utensils. Animatronic bloody-faced werewolves wear chef's hats, moving their robot arms and legs back and forth, as if they're cooking. Little forest elves with freaky ears pop out of steaming pots and pans as we pass by them. They are holding severed heads up. That's what's for dinner, I guess. It looks so real. It's amazing.

I watch Bax. He seems okay. He's looking around at everything, pointing, laughing. The carriage lurches right suddenly, and another set of double doors cracks open: THWANK-WHACK. Now we are in a giant dining room. It's all candle-lit, warm and dim. A fake fire burns in a hearth against the wall. Eerie piano music plays. Little rat robots dance along the mantle. They have red eyes. Fake bats fly overhead, wings flapping. Fake spiders drop from the ceiling and scurry back up again. The long dining room table is covered in dust, and all the people, sitting and eating, are dead. Skeletons. Mummies. They hold forks and knives and look at their plates, which have bloody eyeballs and fingers on them. Gross—why are they eating eyes and fingers? Dead things eat fingers and eyes?

We move through the dining room toward another set of doors. These don't fly open though, because they already are, as if welcoming us. Soon as we go through, the carriage lurches left again—Bax yelps—we both grip the metal bar across our laps to steady ourselves as the lights go out. It's pitch black and smells chemical-sweet, the smell of the smoke haze. Everything starts to glow.

"Cool," Bax says. "Look, Kirbz."

Walls. I think it's a labyrinth. The carriage moves on through it, but every few seconds, a wall shifts, blocking us, until another one opens and lets us through. Some of the walls move toward us quickly, and we yell out, but before they hit the carriage, they stop and then retract. When we finally make it to the end of the maze—no wonder this ride takes so long—big glowing purple words appear above: WITCH'S LABO-RAT-ORY.

The carriage enters a mad scientist's lab with cauldrons and microscopes, bulbous glass containers, trays of tools, and jars stuffed with squishy creatures. A witchy voice rings out: "*Eeee-heee-heee, now deary, you'll make a fine addition to my experiments. How about a nice warm bath? Yes, a bath—IN MY BUBBLING CAULDRON. HA HA HA.*"

Suddenly, a panel on the floor slides open. Haze and green light fill the room, and a huge witch, maybe ten feet tall, rises up slowly from under the floor, her pointy hat tall and glitter-black, a dusty broom in her warty hands. A screeching animatronic rat prances on her shoulder. She makes the Wicked Witch of the West look like a Barbie doll. Her skin glows green and her eyes blaze orange. She mechanically jerks her head toward us in the cart, then lunges aggressively as the lights pop off once again.

Strobe lights start flashing and pumping by the hundreds, thousands, millions. I yelp and cover Bax's eyes. He wrestles free. "Bax, no," I say. "Don't look."

I can't see properly. Only flickers of things between the strobes. It's... it makes me feel dizzy. The witch's long black arms are outstretched, and she reaches for Bax. I try to grab him. Everything looks slow and choppy because of the strobing. And between the flashes, I see him slump forward, then back, then forward, then side to side, and I can't tell if this is…if is this part of the ride. Is he doing this?

No.

He's having one right now.

My heart flip-flops in my chest, playing witchfrog with my other organs. I feel it down in my stomach, thumping and jolting.

Not sure what else to do, so I yell, as loud as I can. I scream out. "Help us," but no one can hear me. Not over the sounds of bubbling, and cackling, and thunder, and scary music. I throw my whole body onto Bax's, trying to stop the thrashing. I hear moans garbling from his mouth. He does this when he has seizures. Doctor-of-Brains says it has to do with his brain trying to get itself working again, like when a hose gets a kink, and you unravel it for the water to flow.

Tears shoot out from my eyes. My hands are shaking. Bax, no. I've only been at home when he's had a seizure. Dad has always been there. This is something else, and I might throw up. The giant evil witch finally retracts into the floor, hissing as she melts. The lights come up again, and the car jostles forward to the next part of the ride. I'm holding onto Bax so hard. I feel wetness, can smell pee. I nudge my fingers into his mouth to make sure he doesn't swallow his tongue— they told us this would happen and to never put anything in his mouth during seizure, but the thought of him swallowing his tongue is too scary. But he's out, as if he's fainted. I'm sweating. I can feel the warm droplets in my eyelashes.

The car moves through a few more rooms, but I can't

pay attention to what's happening. I'm trembling so much, my teeth chatter. I'm yelling at the top of my lungs, but no one can hear me. I try to text Dad, but there's no signal inside this stupid ride. I keep shaking Bax to wake him up, but he won't wake up. I put my ear to his chest to make sure he is breathing. He is. The little car jerks and lurches along on its tracks as we move through some other…what's this? I look around: wait, a bathroom? Ghosts appear in the mirror and disappear again. Almost like the people in the Harry Potter portraits. The faucet turns on and off suddenly, filling the sink with steam. Overhead, hazy light flickers on and off. The walls are a pale green, tiled. A werewolf reading a bloodied newspaper sits on a toilet in the corner, lets out a loud howl.

My hand is clamped hard over Bax's eyes even though he is unconscious, but I'm so scared that he might open them again right as more strobe lights go off. I keep shaking him, hoping he'll wake up. I can smell his orangey shampoo. Hugging him, I squeeze my eyes shut and say, "Please God, get us out of here." I've never said 'Please God' in my entire life.

A second later, the carriage rises on the tracks and clunks through a tube that is basically like the inside of a car wash. Gigantic, colorful fabric strips flail around, whipping and slapping me in the head and face, which would be fun if I wasn't freaking out. I keep Bax covered, protecting him from these weird, heavy blankets thrashing us around. Otherwise he'd be thrown clear out of the cart. My entire body is trembling, I can even feel it in my small toe.

BLAM! We are back outside, in the front, down the line from where we started, a cool rush of wind on my face, and blinking lights, and the smells so strong right now. Pretzels and bubble gum, perfume and hay, beer and hot cheese. I stand up in the carriage and yell out for Dad. He hears me, standing out in the thoroughfare with his friends, turns his head and sees me, smiles and waves.

"No," I yell, "it's Bax. It's bad."

He stares at me for a second, adjusts his glasses, then his face goes slack. He says something over his shoulder to his friends and they all jump up suddenly and run over, fast, shoving people out of the way as they cross the crowded thoroughfare. I sigh, my shaking hand on Baxter's dampened head.

Tears stream down my face.

In the distance, the warbly old-fashioned carnival music prances on the air as the horses on the carousel bow and curtsy, bobbing and diving. A sea of colored steel mares that glide up and down, around and around. Why do they paint such scary faces on carousel horses?

EXCERPT Magazine No. 3

CONTRIBUTORS

Alan Sincic is a teacher at Valencia College. His fiction has appeared in Boulevard Online, New Ohio Review, The Greensboro Review, The Saturday Evening Post, Mid-American Review, Terrain.org, Grist and elsewhere. After an MA in Lit at the University of Florida and a poetry fellowship at Columbia, he earned an MFA at Western New England University. He spent over a dozen years in NYC as a writer and performer—comic/satirical pieces that eventually became a pair of full-length plays (American Obsessions and Breaking Glass) at the Orlando International Fringe Festival. You can visit him at alansincic.com.

Synopsis: Set in the heartland of Depression-era Florida, *The Slapjack* wends its way through the skirmish lines of small-town life to tell, with humor and warmth, the tale of how two loners learn the ways of love. GB is a barefoot boy run-away with a price on his head. Maggie is a beauty embittered by the polio that hobbles her. They meet. They collide. Together they take on the townies who rule the tiny crossroads of Piney Vista. Maggie converts a derelict Feed 'n Seed into a diner and sets out to battle any suitor fool enough to offer her a hand. GB commandeers a cow pasture, a billboard blown over in a hurricane, and a beat-up old army projector to conjure up The Piney Vista Drive-In. She taunts him at every turn but secretly favors him. He scrambles and grifts and bids on whatever piece of property might, somehow, magnify him in her eyes. So begins the dance. Back and forth they go as the years roll by, Maggie fierce in defense of that heart of hers, GB pawing like a bear at the door of love. In a bid to win her over, GB engineers an elaborate scam involving a hurricane, a barbecue, a dare-devil high-diver, and rumors of a spectacular suicide that gathers in the whole of the town to witness the tender, the fierce, the collision of these two most unlikely of lovers.

CONTRIBUTORS

Lindsey Hoshaw's work has appeared in The New York Times, The Boston Globe and on NPR. Lindsey's first-person account of visiting the Great Pacific Garbage Patch was published in "The New Times Book of Science: More Than 150 Years of Groundbreaking Scientific Coverage." *The Night Scorpion*, a thriller set in her hometown of Tucson, Arizona, is her debut novel.

Synopsis: Written in a suspenseful and pithy tone, *The Night Scorpion* is Tokyo Vice set in the Sonoran Desert. In the sweltering summer of 1986, quirky journalist Wren Stevens gets a tip that turns into the story of her career. But as she uncovers dark political secrets and makes inroads with mafioso Sonny Caputo, who's suspected of killing Tucson's mayor, she's quickly in over her head. What starts as blind ambition becomes an unrelenting quest to prove herself and Wren will stop at nothing to expose Sonny, even if it destroys her.

*

J.T. Price's fiction has appeared in The New England Review, Post Road, Guernica, The Heavy Feather Review, Fence, The Brooklyn Rail, and elsewhere. He has served in editorial roles at several lit mags, most recently as editor-in-chief of the Brazenhead Review. In the writing of *A Leading Man*, he consulted more than twenty biographical texts, including an unauthorized biography of Jane Wyman and the ever spirited *Cagney on Cagney*. He can be found online at jt-price.com.

Synopsis: *A Leading Man* is a biographic novel about young Ronald Reagan, and his time as an outspoken progressive in Golden Age Hollywood, as his wife Jane Wyman's career ineluctably supersedes his own.

Drew Buxton is a writer from Texas. His short story collection *So Much Heart* won the Texas Institute of Letters' 2024 Sergio Troncoso Award for Best First Book of Fiction. His work has been featured or is forthcoming in The Drift, SARKA, Joyland, Archway Editions Journal, Electric Literature, and Vice among other publications. Find him at drewbuxton.com.

Synopsis for *Daytona Teddy Riggs*: Set in mid-nineties South Texas, the novel is an offbeat portrayal of mental illness in the pre-internet South, before the possibility of self-diagnosis. Estranged from his oil-rich family who disapprove of his lifestyle, Daytona's primary source of companionship is the Pat Dupree (think Tony Robbins) motivational tapes he listens to on a loop. This opening scene finds Daytona sneaking into a middle school football practice in an effort to relive his former glory.

*

Kurt Baumeister is the author of the novels *Pax Americana* and the forthcoming *Twilight of the Gods* (Stalking Horse Press 2025). An editor with 7.13 Books, his writing has appeared in Salon, Guernica, Electric Literature, and other outlets. Find him on the internet at kurtbaumeister.com.

Synopsis: *Twilight of the Gods* is satire and alternate history on an operatic, cinematic, and cosmic scale, with a cast that transcends time and space. The grinding of The Wheel of Fate is heard in Valhalla, as it is in Berlin and Boston. Can Odin's many schemes be undone? Who can rewire the robotic nightmare of politics and write a brighter future for humanity? Only humanity's champion, the long misunderstood, supposed force of evil, Loki. This is a tale of fallen gods and failing humanity, of love lost and found, magic and sex, art and lies, good, evil, and the end of Fate. This is the story of Loki. In his own words.

CONTRIBUTORS

Tim Cummings is the author of the best-selling coming-of-age novel *Alice the Cat* published by Fitzroy Books/Regal House. He holds an MFA in Creative Writing from Antioch University Los Angeles and a BFA from NYU/Tisch School of the Arts. Recent publications of short fiction, essays, and poetry include F(r)iction, Scare Street, Lunch Ticket, MeowMeow PowPow, From Whispers to Roars, Drunk Monkeys, Hare's Paw, Lit Angels, and Critical Read/RAFT, for which he won the 'Origins' contest for his essay, "You Have Changed Me Forever." His follow-up novel, The Lightning People Play, will be published in the summer of 2024 by Black Rose Writing. www.timcummings.ink | Instagram: octospark

Synopsis: *The Lightning People Play* is a novel forthcoming from Black Rose Writing. Fourteen-year-old Kirby Renton is a gifted theatre kid who wants to fix things, like his dads' marriage and his younger brother's epilepsy. When ten-year-old Baxter's seizures start involving visits from "the lightning people," who descend from the sky and show him strange symbols, Kirby knows he needs to protect his brother, but how? He thinks he's found the answer when the neurologist tells his family to consider a seizure-alert dog, but the cost is too much for his family to afford. Determined to raise the money himself, Kirby enlists his best friends and a crew of brilliant teens from his theatre troupe to put on a play in his epic forest of a backyard. At first, the play brings its own pressures as the drama between Kirby's dads worsens and his fears for his brother climb. But little does Kirby know of the magic that awaits him—and the portal that will open—from his daring to make a difference.

www.ingramcontent.com/pod-product-compliance
Lightning Source LLC
Chambersburg PA
CBHW051307250626
47155CB00009B/3471